PENNY HAD BEEN HAVING THE SAME NIGHTMARE FOR YEARS.

Sometimes in the dream it's a faceless boy who chases her through the woods, dogging her heels easily like a loping predator. In the worst ones he has a knife, a long sharp one, the kind she cut her finger with, and she can see it flashing in the gloom when she looks over her shoulder. She's running down the narrow trail that leads toward the creek, and there he'll be, right on her tail, his sinewy arm reaching for her.

THE CREEK

JENNIFER L. HOLM
THE CREEK

HarperTrophy®
An Imprint of **HarperCollins***Publishers*

Harper Trophy® is a registered trademark of HarperCollins Publishers Inc.

The Creek

Library of Congress Cataloging-in-Publication Data

Holm, Jennifer L.

The creek / by Jennifer L. Holm.—1st ed.

p. cm.

Summary: Around the time of her thirteenth birthday, Penny's suburban Philadelphia neighborhood is terrorized by a psychopath, and everyone is sure that the young man just out of a juvenile home is responsible.

ISBN 0-06-000133-X—ISBN 0-06-000134-8 (lib. bdg.)

ISBN 0-06-000135-6 (pbk.)

[1. Psychopaths—Fiction. 2. Fear—Fiction. 3. Neighborhood—Fiction. 4. Philadelphia (Pa.)—Fiction.] I. Title.

PZ7.H732226Cr 2003   2002010980

[Fic]—dc21   CIP

                                                                              AC

Typography by Karin Paprocki

❖

First Harper Trophy edition, 2004

Visit us on the World Wide Web!

www.harperteen.com

For my mom—
who saw it all

and

For my brother Jon—
who knows what really happened

THE CREEK

ACKNOWLEDGMENTS

There were a number of gracious, supportive people who helped me scare myself to death.

First, I'd like to thank my brother Jon, whose photos remind me what the creek really looked like. Many thanks to Jill Grinberg for her dogged patience, Elise Howard and Clarissa Hutton for their thoughtful criticism, Todd Kessler and Rebecca Goldstein for their enthusiasm, my parents, and my dear friend Wendy Wilson, who keeps me from having panic attacks! As always, many thanks to my brother Matt, who helps me keep everything straight.

I had a lot of doctors helping me out with the details. Many thanks to Jeffrey D. Siegel, M.D.; Alvin Calderon, M.D., Ph.D.; and my favorite pediatrician ever—William Wendell Holm, M.D. A special thanks to a great girl who knows exactly what a dead body looks like—New York City Medical Examiner Judy Melinek, M.D.

Most of all, I must thank my husband, Jonathan, for his unwavering belief in this story. He has been my muse and inspiration. This book would never have been written if he hadn't sat me down at dinner that night and told me *Write, Jenni!*

This book is for all the kids from my childhood who played Chase—wherever you are.

CHAPTER 1

Penny Carson! Get inside this instant and finish your breakfast!" Twelve-year-old Penny Carson shrugged. She knew her mother would call her again in a few minutes. Besides, she had better things to do.

She was sitting on the curb with Mac McHale. They were just killing time in that perfect part of the day, when it was cool and there was still dew on the lawns, before the June heat knocked them over.

School was out, and after a year of bells telling her where to be every minute, it suddenly seemed important to Penny to do nothing. Nothing that required any strenuous thought, and certainly nothing that involved fractions. And sitting on the curb watching Mac fry ants with his new magnifying glass definitely counted as nothing.

Mac had cleverly placed a scrap of toast with jelly

as bait on the ground, and the ants kept on coming despite the fact that their comrades were going up in smoke all around them.

"They're not very smart, are they?" Penny observed.

The sound of a car door opening and slamming shut made Mac hunch his shoulders a little and focus his attention on the sizzling ants.

"Come on, Angus, let's get moving!" a voice rang out. It was Mac's mother. She was the only one Penny had ever heard call him Angus and not be beaten to a pulp.

"Where are you going?" Penny asked.

"Dentist," Mac said in his typically laconic way. Penny felt a little sorry for the dentist.

Solidly built, with a mop of reddish-brown curls and fiery green eyes, twelve-year-old Mac was the undisputed tough guy of their little group, their own private bully. He was always getting into fights, so often that his mother had become friends with the triage nurse at the emergency room.

"Angus, I mean it. Get moving!" Mrs. McHale hollered out the car window. "I don't have time for this." Mrs. McHale was a divorced mother. Mac's dad had left years ago, and Penny never saw him around.

From all accounts, neither did Mac.

Mac looked at the slow-backing station wagon and shrugged in a resigned way.

"Can I borrow the magnifying glass while you're gone?" Penny asked.

Mac narrowed his eyes, considering. "Don't break it." Then he handed the silver-handled beauty over to her.

"I won't," she promised.

"Angus!" Mrs. McHale yelled, her voice rising a notch.

Mac rolled his eyes. "Gotta go. See you at the fort later."

"Right," Penny said.

She watched as Mrs. McHale's station wagon disappeared up Mockingbird Lane, passing cookie-cutter split-level and two-story colonial houses, blacktop driveways, and neatly manicured lawns. Penny turned the shiny magnifying glass over in her hand carefully. The glass was thick, and bulged out like her baby brother Sam's belly.

On the street, the ants were still circling the jelly-covered toast, blindly following one another in manic little lines. She poised the glass over the toast to catch the sun, and as the glass caught the light, she heard the low thick rumbling of a revving engine. She looked up to see a sleek red Trans Am with tinted windows rolling smoothly down Mockingbird Lane as if it had a perfect right to be there.

Penny wondered who the car belonged to. She knew what everyone drove. The last person to buy a new car had been Oren Loew's father, and it was a flashy sort of Jaguar that her mother said he was buying because of a midlife crisis. But the Trans Am was something else. For starters, it wasn't the kind of car a dad would buy, or more to the point, it wasn't the kind of car a mom would *allow* a dad to buy, midlife crisis or not.

She watched its careful progress down the block. With its jacked-up wheels and custom hubcaps, it was a striking contrast to all the tame-looking sedans and minivans in the driveways. It seemed to slow down as it approached, as if casing the block. *Was it a robber?* she wondered nervously. The Albrights' house had been robbed the previous summer when they were down at the Jersey shore, and Benji's little sister, Becky, had had her piggy bank stolen.

The car came to a gentle stop across the street in front of the Bukvics' house, the engine idling. The driver's window rolled down, and a lightly haired masculine hand languidly appeared to flick open an antique-looking silver cigarette case. The nails on the hand were thick with grease, the fingers streaked with grime. Another gritty hand appeared to remove a cigarette and tap it once on the case. And then a lighter was conjured up, a flame sparked. The hand cupped the flame. A head bent, inhaled, lit the waiting cigarette with much-practiced ease. The cigarette glowed in the darkness of the car like a burning eye.

Penny leaned forward, squinting harder, and then she caught sight of the back of that hand—and the skull tattoo. She gasped audibly and dropped the magnifying lens, which struck the curb and shattered.

She had seen a picture of him, years ago.

They had been goofing off, playing at her best friend Amy's house. Amy's mother had been on the phone downstairs, so they had taken the opportunity to sneak into Amy's older brother's room and rifle through the treasures of a fifteen-year-old boy's desk. It was there they had found the small, carefully clipped photo from a newspaper article. It had been tucked in the back of the top drawer, behind piles of rolled-up tube socks. The article had been cut away, but the caption remained:

LOCAL BOY INVOLVED IN ACCIDENT

Penny remembered that photo now, remembered the shape of the boy's head, capped with dark hair, and the thin, worn jean jacket he had been wearing. She remembered how his eyes had stared out at her from that photo, dark and glittering and unreadable. His hand had been curled around something at the edge of the photo, the menacing skull tattoo grinning from the back of his hand.

The same exact tattoo she was looking at right now.

Now, as his head swiveled toward the sound of the breaking magnifying glass, she knew it was him. It had to be.

Caleb Devlin.

"Penny Carson! Get in this house right now and finish your breakfast!" her mother called. "Now!"

The hand in the car flicked a finger, as if dismissing her, and Penny leaped up and ran inside.

Penny's family was already sitting at the breakfast table in the sunny yellow kitchen. Her father was studying the paper, and her mother was spooning baby food into Baby Sam's mouth, or at least trying to. Sam was spitting out every spoonful in a very determined way.

Penny slid into her seat and looked at the plate of scrambled eggs in front of her. Across the table, her brother Teddy was wolfing down his eggs. How could she even think of eating at a time like this? She had just seen Caleb Devlin!

"Teddy!" she hissed.

Teddy looked up sleepily from the open comic book he was reading and stared at her through brown eyes framed by thick glasses. His mousy bowl-cut hair jutted out comically in all directions, tousled from sleep.

"Guess who I just saw?"

"Who?"

"Caleb Devlin!"

Teddy's jaw dropped, revealing a mouthful of scrambled eggs.

"Teddy, close your mouth," her mother said.

His mouth snapped shut like a turtle's, and his face went a little pale. Teddy, at ten, was small for his age, and anxious. "For real?" he mouthed silently.

Penny, whose heart had slowed to a steady thump-thump after the initial shock, nodded. But was she sure? It was like seeing the Loch Ness monster, or Bigfoot. You thought that snaky head in the water was a monster . . . but was it? And Caleb Devlin was worse than a monster. Worse than any vampire or mummy or creepy-crawly slimy creature.

Caleb Devlin, the legendary kid who had terrorized an entire town, had once lived down the street in a shabby-looking ranch house at the end of a long dirt driveway that led off the cul-de-sac. The house had tired reddish-brown siding the color of a hot dog left out too long in the sun. His parents still lived there, but Caleb had been gone for years now, packed off to a juvenile home.

Mr. Cat, Penny's orange tabby, meowed plaintively at the back door.

"Somebody please let the cat out," her mother said, looking at Penny.

Penny groaned.

Her pediatrician father shook himself from the paper and looked at Penny, trying to assume a stern expression. "Listen to your mother, Penny. Be a good girl or there won't be any surprises on your birthday."

Her birthday was next week and she was looking forward to it. She had requested a new bicycle—had ripped out a picture of the one she wanted and put it on her mother's tiny desk by the kitchen phone. It was hot pink, with a handlebar brake, cool orange reflectors, and a bright, shiny horn. Penny had been riding her mother's old three-speed for the past year. It was an ugly army-surplus shade of green, and the gears always got stuck in second.

Penny had a pretty good feeling that she was going to get the bike. She had certain things going for her, after all. As the oldest child and only girl, she didn't have to suffer hand-me-downs like Baby Sam eventually would. She had her own bedroom, with pink dotted-swiss curtains and a canopy bed. Penny suspected that the bike was already in the storage shed behind the house, waiting for the big day.

Mr. Cat meowed louder, his tail rising in a threatening way that said he was going to do something bad on the carpet if someone didn't let him out soon.

"Penny, it's your cat, and if I have to clean up that carpet one more time, he's going back to the pound," her mother said, shooting her a look that said she meant business.

Penny got up and walked over to the screen door, where Mr. Cat was meowing madly. The cat caught sight of Penny and purred. She knelt down and scratched him behind the ears.

"Good cat," Penny said.

She opened the screen door and he streaked out into the backyard, dissolving into the dark shadows of the woods behind the house. Despite loving Penny, Mr. Cat sometimes disappeared for days at a time before wandering home for a cuddle and a free meal. There were a lot of orange kittens in the neighborhood, and her mother said Penny should have named the cat Mr. Gigolo.

"Mom . . . ," Penny said, sliding back into her seat.

Across the table, Baby Sam spit out a chunk of baby food with a happy gurgle.

"Come on, sweetie," her mother begged desperately, waving a spoon at Baby Sam's open mouth.

"Mom . . . ," Penny said. The stupid baby took up every single second of her mother's attention, and lately she wondered if her mother even knew that she still lived in the house.

"What, Penny?" her mother said absently.

"What did Caleb do that got him sent away?" Penny asked.

Her parents exchanged a look.

"Gotta go, hon. See you tonight. If the answering service calls, I'm at the hospital doing rounds, so have them beep me." Her father abruptly stood up, grabbing his white lab coat. He was out the kitchen door.

"Mom?" Penny pressed.

"I honestly have no idea, Penny. He was already gone when we moved here," her mother demurred, wiping the baby's mouth with a towel. It looked disgusting, with dribbled milk and baby food.

The phone rang shrilly.

"One of you kids get that," Mrs. Carson ordered, her attention firmly fixed on Baby Sam.

Penny leaped up to get the phone. "Hello?"

She held out the cordless phone. "It's Mrs. Bukvic, Mom," Penny said. Mrs. Bukvic lived across the street and was Amy's mother.

Her mother sighed and said, "All right, bring me the phone."

Penny sat back down and pretended to pay attention to her eggs. Her mother was trying to spoon some gross-looking food into Baby Sam's mouth at the same time as she talked to Mrs. Bukvic.

"Hi, Betty Ann," her mother said in a bright sort of voice, wedging the phone between her ear and shoulder. "Yes, it's chaos here, as usual. How are things at work?" A pause and then, "You saw who? Caleb Devlin?"

Penny met Teddy's eyes across the table. It *had* been him after all!

The stories flashed through her mind—the ones that were whispered on playgrounds at recess, between innings at softball games, at the bus stop before school. None of the kids knew all the exact details, but legend had it that Caleb was responsible for more than one mysterious death in the neighborhood. As if by some unspoken agreement, the parents refused to discuss it.

Their mother was saying, "Really, Betty Ann, I just can't believe all that spooky stuff," her voice trailing off into a whisper as she realized that Teddy and Penny were listening. "Let me call you back later, after I put the baby down. Okay? Great. 'Bye." Their mother switched off the phone and put it on the table, looking at Teddy and Penny.

"Uh, Mom," Penny asked in a careful voice, "did Mrs. Bukvic say that Caleb was back?"

Her mother gave her a long look. "Penny, don't let your superstitions run away with you. He's just a boy."

Penny shook her head firmly. "No way, Mom. Caleb's really bad. Everyone says so."

Teddy nodded in agreement. "Yeah, Mom, everybody knows that."

Her mother shook her head, her straw-colored hair, long like a teenager's, gleaming in the warm kitchen light. At thirty-two, Mrs. Carson was younger than the other moms, and she was cool, as much as a mom could be cool. The kids who had working mothers, like Mac, jostled to hang out at the Carson house after school and drink the root beer floats she made. Her mother's coolness was elevated by the fact that she sometimes played video games with them, and was pretty good at the driving ones.

"Yeah," Penny said, pressing her point. "He must have done something for them to send him away."

But her mother was already back to trying to feed Baby Sam. She elaborately flew a spoon of strained peaches toward the baby's mouth, swooping it like an airplane. "I think Caleb got into a really bad fight with some boy," she said distractedly, as if it was no big thing, as if being sent away to reform school was something that happened to kids every day.

"I knew it," Penny said, feeling vindicated.

"Penny, it was a long time ago. And he was just a young kid then. Lots of boys get into fights." She winked at Teddy. "Even you, young man."

The ghost of a smile appeared on Teddy's solemn face.

Her mother leaned forward and pushed the spoon gently against Baby Sam's lips, but he just gave her a gooey grin, mouth firmly shut. Nothing was getting past this kid.

"But, Mom, Caleb's really dangerous!" Penny said.

Her mother looked at the baby in frustration, sat back, and pushed the hair off her forehead, clearly at wit's end. "Do you remember when we were living in Philadelphia and that boy pulled a gun on us when we were doing the laundry?"

Penny nodded. They had been in the small, steamy Laundromat down the street from their third-story walk-up apartment. Her mother had been folding her father's underwear when a skinny boy with a red knit cap had held a gun to her back and demanded all her money, especially quarters. Penny had wondered if he'd wanted quarters so that he could play pinball in the pizza parlor down the block.

"Now, *that* was dangerous. Nothing like that happens here. That's why your dad and I decided to move here," her mother said in a reassuring voice, absently stirring the baby food in the jar. "This is the suburbs, Penny."

"But, Mom," Penny insisted.

"People get spooked by the littlest things out here because it's so safe. You have nothing to fear. It's all silly talk." Her mother expertly pushed a spoonful of baby food into Sam's mouth. The baby promptly spit it out, the chunk landing with a distinct wet splat on the tray table.

"But—" Penny said.

"Sam!" her mother cried.

"Mom!"

Her mother was frantically wiping up the baby food, a harried look on her face. "Listen, you two, people like to gossip, especially in small towns. They say bad things about other people. But that doesn't always mean they're true. You can't believe everything you hear. Mrs. Devlin is very sick, and I'll bet Caleb is just home to visit. I really don't think his family needs to hear anything like this at such a time. So I don't want to hear either of you spreading rumors about Caleb Devlin, all right?" She spoke too fast, her voice high, the way it always sounded when she was about to lose her temper.

"But even Mrs. Bukvic knows that Caleb is bad!"

Her mother sighed heavily. "Well, Mrs. Bukvic isn't your mother, and I am. Got it?"

Baby Sam, sitting in his high chair, kicked his feet, diverting their mother's attention back to the task at hand.

"All right, now. Let's get your little brother fed

before he wastes away to nothing," her mother said in a determined voice.

Penny thought that was pretty unlikely. Baby Sam resembled a plump pink piglet.

"Come on, now, be a good baby," her mother begged. Baby Sam opened his mouth a crack, and her mother quickly shoved a spoonful of peach baby food into his mouth.

"Good baby!" Mrs. Carson clapped. She turned to Penny and Teddy and hissed, "Clap, you two. We have to encourage him."

Penny and Teddy rolled their eyes and clapped, and Baby Sam, amused, smiled broadly.

"Good baby!" their mother said like a cheerleader.

Baby Sam hiccuped once and then, incredibly, barfed down the front of his bib and clean duck-yellow snuggly suit, across the short tray table, and all over the front of their mother's white T-shirt, leaving a kaleidoscope of peach baby food and something that was green and smelled like old peas.

For a moment everything was quiet, and then Teddy broke the silence.

"That," he said in awe, "was really cool."

CHAPTER 2

Penny stepped out of the house. At that same exact moment, Amy Bukvic stepped out from her own front door across the street.

Amy was fourteen, a year and a half older than Penny, and she was wearing a pair of tight jeans and a top that accentuated her burgeoning chest. Her auburn hair was arranged in a deliberately casual style that brushed across her face, making her look mysterious and grown-up.

"Going to play with the boys?" she asked in a mocking voice.

Penny didn't know what to say. That was exactly what she was going to do.

"Uh, yeah. Want to come? We're gonna—"

Amy held up a finger. "Wait, don't tell me." She pretended to think very hard. "You're going to build

17

a fort in the woods?"

"Right," Penny said awkwardly. "Want to come?"

Acres of undeveloped woods ringed the houses of Mockingbird Lane on both sides, and it was here that the kids of the block built a tree fort every summer. Two years ago, Amy had helped with the fort herself. She had painted one of the walls pink, much to the boys' collective dismay. Still, it had been fun.

Amy laughed. "You couldn't pay me to play with those dirtball boys in the woods. When are you gonna grow up, huh, Penny? You're so stupid."

Penny felt tears prick at the back of her eyelids, felt the way her chest got tight. "I'm not stupid," she said in a shaking voice.

Amy yawned widely and adjusted a lacy bra strap, as if she was too bored to respond.

"I'm not!" Penny whispered.

"Get lost," Amy said with casual cruelty.

Penny turned and fled back into the house.

The creek curled and twisted like a lazy snake through the woods, and like a snake, it was deadly in places, with high cliffs overlooking the thin thread of muddy brown water and sharp stones. Elsewhere, it opened into broad flats that were filled with dry, smooth stones, where the water swelled from bank to bank after a hard rain.

This year, it had been decided that the fort would be built on a stretch of low embankment overlooking the creek less than a hundred yards from the back of Mac's house. The creek wound behind the left side of Mockingbird Lane, as you faced the cul-de-sac— the side Mac's and Penny's families lived on—before shooting off into the depths of the woods, where its banks grew increasingly steep and treacherous. A bunch of older boys had built a fort on this same location several years back, and it had been well known as a favorite place for make-out sessions. Rumor had it that Caleb Devlin had taken over the fort before being sent away.

The original support beams were still there, stretched perilously between three pine trees, almost fifteen feet up, hanging over the edge of the creek. It was every mother's nightmare. The appeal was undeniable.

Penny stood there, looking at the beams high in the trees, wondering how much it would hurt if you fell from such a height. A lot, she decided.

"We need lumber," Benji Albright said. Benji, who had sandy hair, a freckled face, and a huge gap between his front teeth, was a scrapper, the first to dive in, to break a tooth, to bloody a nose. Both he and Mac had been in Penny's homeroom, and it had seemed like the year had been one long fistfight.

"There's some at the skeet range," Mac said.

"How do we get it?" Benji asked.

"We steal it," Mac said, like Benji was stupid.

"I don't know," Benji said.

"Well, I do, so shut up," Mac said.

Mac was good at this sort of thing. Good at knowing when to sneak into the firing range to steal skeets, and when there were vacant houses in the neighborhood to explore. Last summer he had netted a huge box of pink bathroom tiles that had been left behind in a basement when a family up the block moved out. Not that tiles were good for much, but it was a score in any case. Petty theft was a skill.

Stealing aside, Penny was pretty sure that building a fort on the same spot as Caleb Devlin's old fort was more than stupid, especially considering what she'd just heard at breakfast. It seemed like bad luck to her, like building on a haunted graveyard. Penny eyed the spot of the proposed fort warily. Dense limbs cast lacy shadows, and the air smelled green and mossy, with an undercurrent of decay from rotting wood. The ground seemed darker around the trees, and there was something else, something she was having a harder time putting her finger on. And then it struck her.

There was nothing growing on the spot—no flowers, no wild ferns, not even the oniony sort of weed that grew everywhere in the dark, humid woods. Where were the birds? Why weren't there any birds up in the trees? It didn't make sense.

Unless, she thought suddenly, maybe the ghosts of Caleb's victims were still here, lurking around, killing plants and scaring away animals. Bad things didn't go away easily, Penny knew.

Penny was superstitious. She knocked on wood, always threw salt over her shoulder when it spilled, and never stepped on cracks. And other things, too. She never, *ever*, killed praying mantises, and she always carefully carried crickets outside when she found them in the house. She had learned these superstitions from her grandmother, Nana, who lived in Key West, ·Florida.

"Penny," Teddy said, tugging her hand anxiously. "Tell them."

Penny swallowed hard. "You guys, did you hear?"

"Hear what?" Benji said.

"Caleb's back."

It was hot out, so hot that their skin was slick with little beads of sweat, but Penny's words caused them to shiver where they stood.

"What?" Oren Loew said, his voice a croak. Oren, who had just turned thirteen, was the oldest of the boys. The only Jewish kid on the block, and the most responsible, Oren was experiencing some mild embarrassment from his changing voice. Puberty had its tight grip on his throat, and his face was a rash of pimples.

"Says who?" Mac demanded, starting to go red, his voice full of anger. He was in a foul temper, but then, the dentist could do that to a person. "And where's my magnifying glass?"

"I saw him myself," Penny said in a solemn voice.

Penny was many things—an excellent shortstop, a good climber, a fair spitter, a girl—but she was not a liar.

"But do you even know what he looks like?" Mac asked, not convinced.

"I saw the tattoo. The skull tattoo on the back of his hand," she said.

That shut them all up. They stared at each other in silence.

"Maybe it has something to do with his mom,"

Oren said thoughtfully, his thick black curls catching bits of light, making them look blue. Oren was like this; he reasoned things out. He was the one who could be counted on to talk everyone down when they got crazy ideas. "I heard my mom on the phone saying that Mrs. Devlin was really sick."

"Caleb's probably what? Seventeen now?" Benji asked.

"He was a grade behind Toby," Mac said. Toby was Mac's older brother, who was off at college. "And he was sent away when he was thirteen."

Oren said, "Yeah, I remember. We were in Miss Simmons's class."

Benji nodded. "Second grade."

It was little things like this that made Penny feel like she would never really fit in, these casual references to things in the past that seemed of great importance, that had become accepted history on the block. Like the time Benji had broken his leg in two places when he'd crashed his bike into a ravine, and the time Mac had rigged a remote-control model airplane with firecrackers so that it exploded right in the middle of the Bukvics' annual barbecue. Penny knew these stories like she knew the stories of her own life. But they were borrowed memories.

The Carsons had moved to Mockingbird Lane from Philadelphia three years ago, and while the kids counted her and Teddy as part of the pack, Penny felt that she had to listen harder, try harder, so that her being here could one day be effortless. It was a constant source of worry to her. Her mom was always telling her and Teddy to think for themselves. But Penny knew that it was more important to fit in, and that fitting in generally involved agreeing with everyone else. She didn't want to end up like one of those kids at recess who always sat off to the side, never picked for a game of kickball.

"Man," Mac said with a low whistle. "Remember all those stories?"

"Yeah! Nicky Kapoor told me his brother told him that Caleb showed him an old silver cigarette case. He said he'd stolen it off a sleeping bum," Benji said.

"I saw that case!" Penny said excitedly. "And I saw the skull tattoo on his hand!"

Benji nodded sagely. "Sure sounds like him. But you know that cigarette case?"

The kids waited expectantly, hearts pounding.

Benji's voice pitched low. "They say that case is full of pinky fingers from kids who tried to cross him." A beat, and then he added, "Caleb cut 'em off with his hunting knife."

"That's a steaming load of horse——" Mac started to say.

"I'm not saying it's true," Benji shot back. "My point is, he must have been pretty bad."

"Oh, yeah, why's that?"

"'Cause look at all the bad stuff *you* do, and you never got sent away!"

"That's 'cause *I'm* too smart to get caught!" Mac shouted back in aggravation.

"Pinky fingers does sound a little extreme," Oren said. "But you know they say that he used to set traps here in the woods," he added, looking around at the leaf-covered forest floor. His eyes clouded over. "We never did find Bozo."

"Bozo?" Penny asked.

"Our dog. He was a dachshund. Caleb liked to steal people's pets right out of their yards and kill them in the woods. I know he got Bozo," Oren said with absolute conviction. "He wasn't the kind of dog to run away."

"Bozo?" Mac snorted. "That dog probably killed itself because of its lame name. I bet it sat by the road all day and ran in front of a car when it saw its chance."

"You jerk!" Oren said, flinging himself at Mac.

Benji wrestled him away, and Oren glared at Mac.

"This is serious," Penny said. "I don't think we should build the fort here, because of Caleb and all."

"Forget that. I'd like to see him try and mess with me," Mac said, his fists clenching and unclenching in a menacing way.

Benji gave a pained look. "Yeah, the summer just started. We don't even know for sure if he's back in town."

"But I saw him!"

Mac narrowed his eyes at her. "Are you sure you saw him?"

"He was driving a red Trans Am and—"

"Look," Mac said. "If he was driving a car like that, we'd see it parked in the Devlins' driveway, and I haven't seen one."

"Maybe he just got here this morning!"

"Maybe you're just seeing things," Mac said bluntly. "And where's my magnifying glass?"

"I—I broke it," Penny confessed.

"Typical. You are such a girl," Mac spit out furiously.

"I didn't mean to!"

"Whatever," Mac said. "Let's go."

She took in the stubborn set of the boys' eyes, even Teddy's. "But Caleb——" Penny said.

Mac cut her off.

"I'm sick of hearing about him, so just shut up. We've got a fort to build."

The day was hot and sticky as a melted doughnut.

They had broken for lunch, and reassembled on the storm drain next to Benji's house at the end of the cul-de-sac. Heat hung thick and heavy in the suburban air, and sprinklers were on up and down Mockingbird Lane. Penny's lime-green shorts and tank top were already damp and clinging to her skin. It was not, in Penny's opinion, the ideal time to be doing anything as strenuous as stealing lumber. She tucked her dirty-blond hair behind her ears, happy that she'd cut it short, even though her mom hadn't liked the idea at the time. It was much cooler.

"Are you sure this is a good idea?" Penny asked Mac.

"Yeah," Mac said nonchalantly. "It's been sitting there forever. Nobody'll miss it."

Penny doubted this very much. Somebody would miss it. It was just a question of when.

Just then, Zachary Evreth rode up on his bike, his plump legs pumping furiously. He screeched to a halt and dropped his bike, breathing hard, racing to catch up with them, baseball cards and rubber balls and all sorts of junk falling out of his pockets and onto the ground. He seemed to be carrying everything he owned stuffed into his straining jeans.

"Just what we need!" Benji groaned.

Twelve-year-old Zachary was one of those kids.

With his intense eyes and thin hair, he was too fat, too eager to please, too everything. He was the kid who couldn't keep a secret, the kid who always got hurt at recess, the kid who laughed too long at your jokes, the kid who would never leave you alone.

The kid, in short, who gave other kids a bad name.

"What are you guys doing?" he asked eagerly, all smiles, the human Labrador.

"Stealing wood from behind the skeet range for the new fort," Teddy said.

Penny shot her brother an exasperated look.

"Great, Teddy, why don't you tell the whole world?" Mac said.

Zachary rushed to reassure them. "I won't tell," he said. You could just see his mind whirring. "I can help! I can be, like, the lookout! Huh? What do you think, guys?"

The kids cast sidelong glances at one another.

"I can help!" Zachary pleaded.

"No, it's cool, man," Mac said, nodding his head. "Thanks anyway." He started walking toward the woods, the other boys following.

Zachary's face fell, tears welling up in his eyes.

Penny suddenly felt sorry for the kid. "Next time," she promised, meeting his stricken eyes.

"C'mon, Penny!" Benji shouted.

She ran to catch up.

The skeet range was deep in the woods, behind the Albrights' house. A small dirt road led to it from Wren Circle, but they didn't want to draw any attention to themselves by going that way. The children were forbidden to go to the range, which made no sense, as most of their fathers owned guns and practiced on the range themselves. The fathers were big hunters and often took the boys hunting.

Most of the Mockingbird Lane boys had BB guns, too, even Zachary—which Teddy took as a personal insult, because he didn't have one. Dr. Carson refused to let Teddy have a BB gun because he said he had treated too many gunshot wounds during his residency in Philadelphia, which Teddy thought was unfair because even Oren had a BB gun, and his father was a gastroenterologist.

The boys were generally up to no good with their BB guns. Most of the time they'd set up cans as targets, but sometimes they'd go after squirrels or dumb, slow-moving mourning doves. Penny often thought she should learn how to use a gun despite her parents' strict instructions that she never touch one.

The skeet range was deserted when they reached it, and as Mac had predicted, there was a large pile of wooden beams leaning against the chain-link fence that ringed the range. The boys whooped at the find.

Benji gave a low whistle. "It's like walking into a store."

"Are you sure about this, Mac?" Oren asked hesitantly, clearly leery of committing a crime even if it was for the good of the fort.

"It's cool," said Mac dismissively.

Penny idly admired a tree that kids over the years had carved graffiti on. Mickey loved Carrie. A jagged lightning bolt. Names of bands. A crooked-looking heart. It was like a taunt to the block's fathers. *Look how close we are to the range,* the graffiti said.

"Let's take a load now and then come back for more tomorrow," Mac ordered. It was getting late, nearly five, and their mothers would be hollering for them to come home for dinner soon.

They divvied up into pairs and carried the two-by-fours, except Mac, who made a show of throwing a couple over his shoulder and carrying them by himself. It was a long haul through the twisting trees as the kids followed the Indian trails. Legend had it that the woods had originally been home to the Lenni Lenape and that they were the ones who had left the dirt paths that crisscrossed all over the woods. Penny's father said that it was more likely fifty years of children's feet that had beaten the well-worn paths.

When she and Benji arrived at the fort, lagging behind the others, they dumped their load and relaxed.

Mac and Teddy had Mac's Swiss Army knife out. Penny watched in horror as Teddy threw it up into the air over his head. It landed with a thump on the ground behind his back, point first.

"Teddy!" she shouted, on her feet instantly. "What are you doing!"

"It's just a game," he whined.

"Haven't you ever played this before?" Mac asked. "It's called Dive Bomb."

"It should be called Stupid, that's what!" she said.

"Knives are really dangerous."

"Chill out, Penny," Mac said, but he put the knife away.

"That's a really dumb game." Penny was getting worked up. "I nearly cut my finger off with a knife once, helping Mom. Look!" She held up her forefinger, the white scar a snaking line around pink skin. "I had to have ten stitches!"

"Okay, okay, chill out," Teddy echoed, embarrassed.

"Yeah, go bake some cookies with the other moms," Mac said sourly. "What's your problem, anyway?"

"She has a thing about knives," Benji said under his breath.

Penny grabbed Teddy by his hand and tugged him away from the other boys.

"What if it landed on your head? Use your brain, Teddy," Penny said, admonishing him.

Teddy swallowed. "You think it's okay to build the fort here?" he whispered, so that the other boys wouldn't hear him. He looked around with worried eyes.

This was typical Teddy. He was all fearless bravado when the boys were around, but when it was just the two of them, he let his fears show.

His real question hung in the air, unspoken between them. Teddy feared Caleb Devlin like they all did, but he was not like Benji Albright or Mac McHale. He was not scrappy. He was easily hurt and scared when out of the circle of their rough, confident influence.

"It'll be fine, Teddy," Penny said automatically.

She stared into the woods, squinting slightly, looking past the big fallen oak as the late afternoon sun cast dappled shadows, and she imagined she could see the brooding boy from the car, glaring at her with dead eyes, his skin gleaming with sweat and dirt, the heat rising off his body, the musky smell of danger. Caleb Devlin. She could almost see him standing there, leaning against the sturdy pine tree, grinding marijuana into his cheap rolling papers, inhaling deeply, taunting her, scaring her, scaring them all.

She blinked twice and he was gone.

Mac carried a pile of boards over to where Benji was hammering and dropped them at Benji's feet. One of the boards hit Benji's foot.

"You jerk," Benji said, glaring at Mac. Fighting and bickering were a way of life with the boys, Penny knew. It wasn't personal; it was just something they did.

Mac snickered. He loved a fight. But then he looked up, past Benji, and his smirk turned to a scowl. "Look who's coming," Mac said scornfully.

They spotted her way down the trail. It was Becky Albright, Benji's six-year-old sister, a picture with her curly white-blond hair, robin's-egg-blue eyes, and hand-smocked dress. She clutched a doll in her clean pink hands. Penny thought she looked like a china doll come to life.

Benji shook his head and gave a harassed-sounding groan. "Becky, go home."

"I wanna go up in the fort," she wailed.

"You're too small," Benji said, exasperated. "It's not even finished. It's just beams."

Becky considered, looking up at the raw beams suspended in the trees. "But I wanna."

"No way, Becky, get lost," Benji said. Becky was the bane of Benji's existence. "Don't be a pain."

"I'll tell Mom you went to the range," she threatened. "I saw!" Becky was no dummy; she knew all the right buttons to push.

"Yeah? Well, I'll tell her you're the one who spilled the ice cream on the living-room rug."

"But I wanna go up," she said babyishly.

"Tough," Benji said. "Go home and stop spying on me."

"Yeah, get out, bratty Becky," said Mac.

And then all of them started shouting, "Bratty

Becky, Bratty Baby Becky!" and she began to cry.

"C'mon, Becky," Penny said, snatching the little girl's hand. "I'll take you home. Leave the boys alone." Becky wasn't so bad. She was just a little girl.

Penny led Becky out of the labyrinth of woods and up to the storm drain at the cul-de-sac where Becky promptly started crying harder, dramatically, knowing that Mrs. Albright was within hearing distance.

"Becky, don't get them in trouble or they'll never let you play with them," Penny said in a low voice.

"They're so mean to me! I hate them!" Her face was all red and sort of scrunched up. Penny understood why the boys wouldn't let Becky play with them. It was like baby-sitting.

Penny wiped Becky's nose and gave her a shove in the direction of her house, and then she started back up the block toward her own.

CHAPTER 3

That evening, Penny was sitting on the curb in front of her house with the guys, waiting for Oren to show up. Oren's family always ate dinner late, at seven, so everyone had to wait until he was finished before embarking on any evening activities. Tonight they were going to play flashlight tag.

"This is such a pain," Benji groused. "Why don't they eat dinner at six like normal people?"

Mac grunted in a noncommittal way. He was using a stick to push around a frog that had been dead for some time. It was flat and looked a little crusty around the edges, as if it had been run over by a steam engine and then grilled on a barbecue. It didn't smell so hot, either.

"How could someone run over a frog?" Penny asked, feeling a little queasy.

"My mom once ran over a turtle," Mac said, looking across the street to where his mother was sitting on the Bukvics' porch with Mrs. Albright and Mrs. Bukvic.

The three women were deep in conversation, glancing up occasionally to eye the kids. They were probably organizing the annual Fourth of July block party, Penny thought. The Fourth of July was a big deal on Mockingbird Lane. The day-long block party featured tons of food, kegs of beer for the grown-ups, and contests and games. They were all looking forward to it in a few short weeks.

Mrs. Bukvic was in charge of the block party this year, which was perfect because Mrs. Bukvic was probably the bossiest person on the block.

A police car drove slowly down the street.

"It's the fuzz patrol," Mac said under his breath, acting cool.

For a brief moment Penny worried that the police were coming to get them because someone found out they'd stolen wood from the skeet range.

The car slowed as it passed, and Officer Cox, a balding, round-faced man with splotchy red cheeks, leaned out the window and gave the kids a big smile.

"Hi, kids," he said. "You guys keeping cool? Staying

out of trouble?" His eyes lingered on Mac when he said "trouble."

Mac gave a fake showy smile and said, in a syrupy voice, "Everything's just swell, Officer."

Officer Cox narrowed his eyes.

"Hi, Officer Cox," Penny said, deflecting the attention away from Mac. Penny liked Officer Cox. He came to her school once a year and gave them lectures on being safe and about how they should never get into a car with strangers. He had a nice smile, a smile that said he was a trustworthy person.

"You having a good summer, Penny?" he asked, killing the engine.

"So far."

Mrs. Bukvic came striding over, still wearing heels and a dressy blouse, her plump arms swinging, her little white toy poodle Buster yipping away at her heels. Mrs. Bukvic was a paralegal at a law firm, which was why until recently Amy had always spent afternoons after school at Penny's house. But ever since Amy turned fourteen in December, she was allowed to stay at home by herself, and she ignored Penny completely.

Following behind Mrs. Bukvic were Mrs. Albright and Mrs. McHale.

"Why, hello, Officer Cox," Mrs. Bukvic said sweetly, a tabloid reporter buttering up her victim.

"Ma'am," he said politely.

"And how is your sweet wife?" Mrs. Bukvic asked.

"Vicki's fine, thanks for asking."

"And little Jack?"

"Jack's doing fine, too. Starting third grade next year."

"Well, isn't that lovely," Mrs. Bukvic cooed. She turned to the other women. "Isn't that just lovely, girls?" They made murmuring sounds of agreement.

Mrs. Bukvic lowered her voice. "Have you given any thought to that little problem I called you about?"

Officer Cox regarded her with a level gaze. "Unless there's been a crime committed, there's nothing I can do."

"Typical," Mrs. McHale muttered in disgust, shaking her head. Her curly hair was the same color as Mac's, but on her it looked brassy. "Nobody did anything last time, either, and you remember what happened then!"

"And he's definitely back," Mrs. Bukvic said.

Mrs. Albright pressed forward, hands together. Benji's mom was a petite woman, and sweet. She gave the kids big glasses of lemonade and homemade cookies when they went to her house. She was the opposite of Mrs. McHale, who was always on a diet and kicked the kids out of the house whenever she was dating a new man, which was all the time. She had once gone out with the Phys Ed teacher, which had infuriated Mac to no end.

"Everyone knows that Ruthie's sick," Mrs. Albright said reasonably. "They probably let him out to come visit her."

Mrs. Bukvic nodded in a way that said she had the inside scoop. She looked around and whispered, dramatically, *"Cancer."*

Officer Cox nodded wearily. "I can't do a thing."

The women eyed him with scorn. Buster yipped as if in agreement.

Mrs. Albright jockeyed forward and said, in a soft, urgent voice, "But these children play in the woods." Her voice lowered a notch. "Caleb's a dangerous boy."

A warbling voice came over the car's CB radio, and Officer Cox grabbed the mike desperately.

"Butch here," he said. He listened for a moment, grunted. He turned to Mrs. Bukvic. "I appreciate your concern, and I'll keep an eye on things, but that's all I can do at this point."

Mrs. Bukvic looked panicky. "But Officer Cox, it's

your job to protect us! You know what that boy is capable of!"

Butch Cox looked over at Penny and the boys perched on the curb, and seemed to shudder for a moment. Then he turned back to the mothers and said, with genuine regret, "I know, Betty Ann, but my hands are tied until—"

"Until that demon does something we'll regret for the rest of our lives!" Mrs. Bukvic interjected hotly. She turned on her heel and stormed back to her house, her dog getting in one final yip before trotting after her.

Officer Cox started up his car and drove down around the cul-de-sac and back up the street, quickly, not even bothering to heed the stop sign at the corner.

The remaining mothers eyed the kids like a pair of wrathful goddesses.

Mrs. Albright wagged a finger at them all. "You kids are to stay out of those woods, and away from that creek."

"But, Mom," Benji protested.

"No way," Mac said, immediately regretting his words.

Mrs. McHale looked at him sternly. "That goes for you, too, mister," she said in a firm voice, her curls bobbing in emphasis. "Or else."

Mac lowered his head like a beaten dog. "Yes, ma'am," he whispered.

The women turned and walked back to their respective homes.

"Just great," Mac hissed.

"Do we have to listen to *your* mom?" Teddy asked, confused. "She's not our mom, right, Penny?"

Penny didn't say anything. She was deeply shaken by the reactions of the other moms; it confirmed that her fears were well-grounded.

"This is what we get for waiting for Oren," Mac muttered angrily.

Oren came skateboarding down the block. He ground the back of his board to a stop and flipped it up expertly. "What was that all about?" he asked.

Mac glared at him.

Penny had been having the same nightmare for years.

She's running through the woods and there is a monster chasing her, right on her heels, so close she can feel his breath tickle the nape of her neck. But something holds her back, slows her down— something like Teddy, who can't keep up with her because he's too small, or Baby Sam, who is too heavy to carry, who she ends up half dragging along the forest floor, pine needles catching in his footie pajamas. The real nightmare becomes keeping Teddy or Sam with her and not abandoning them to the force chasing her, because without them she'd be able to run like the wind. She is that fast. But with her brothers, it is like she is running with cement shoes, every step hard; they hold her back. She wakes up just as the monster has almost reached her, just as she feels the cold dead tendrils creeping around her shoulders, trying to pull her down, drag her into the black depths.

Sometimes in the dream it's a faceless boy who chases her through the woods, dogging her heels easily like a loping predator. In the worst ones he has a knife, a long sharp one, the kind she cut her finger with, and she can see it flashing in the gloom when she looks over her shoulder. She's running down the narrow trail that leads toward the creek, and there he'll be, right on her tail, his sinewy arm reaching for her, his cigarette breath hot on her cheek.

And then she would wake up, wanting to scream, flailing for the switch of her bedside lamp. Too scared to go back to sleep again, she would stay up until dawn reading comics until she knew for sure that nothing could hurt her here in this safe, warm house, in her pink room with the canopy bed, with Georgie the bear beside her.

Whenever she had these nightmares, Penny thought of Nana, of what she would say. Nana said that there were things no one could stop. Life was a force of nature, a hurricane, a riptide. The only thing you could do, Nana said, was look at the sky and watch out for storms and, of course, hope your roof didn't blow away.

Nana told Penny these things at her house in Key West, with its wraparound porch infested by termites. She told Penny these things over sweet tea laced with honey as they sat on the swing watching the sunset, the famous Key West sunset. *That was the best sunset,* they said every time, no matter what.

Nana was old, nearly eighty, and everyone agreed that old Nana was sharp as a tack. Her hair was the color of tarnished pewter and her hands were gnarled with arthritis, but she always cooked a Key lime pie with meringue topping when Penny came to visit.

Penny went to Key West to stay with Nana every summer at the same time, the week before school started. Just Penny—not Teddy. "Just us girls," Nana liked to say. No boys allowed.

Every morning when she was in Key West, the first thing Penny did was shake out her shoes. Nana told her to do this: shake out your shoes. Penny wondered about it, but Nana just shook her head, and said, "You'll see, dear, you'll see."

One morning last summer, Penny was shaking out her shoes as usual when out plopped a shiny black scorpion. It waved its claws at her like a miniature demon, and Penny screamed. Nana came running, but by then it was gone, disappeared, under the old iron bed.

"See, Penny," Nana said. "Scorpions like to live near you, where they can do you the most harm. You have to be careful. You have to think like a scorpion. You have to shake your shoes out."

Penny was remembering all these things as she hid in the storm drain. The storm drain was at the end of the cul-de-sac, the lowest point on Mockingbird Lane. Underneath, there was a rectangular space large enough for several kids to stand up in. At the back a long corrugated pipe, big enough to crawl through, opened out into a gully in the woods near the Devlins' house. The pipe had once had a grate on the end to keep out small animals—and children—but some enterprising teenagers had cut it off years ago. It was one of her favorite places—cool despite the summertime heat, redolent with the pungent smell of dried leaves. It was a perfect hiding place for flashlight tag; she'd been sitting there for nearly a half hour now, and no one had found her yet. She shifted her rear end on the corrugated metal grooves, trying to get comfortable.

Penny usually liked flashlight tag. It was a tradition of summer, like swimsuits and corn on the cob and fireflies. And she was good at it, maybe because she didn't mind the dark, not like Teddy who was terrified, who had to go to bed with a night-light on and the door to his room opened a crack.

She flicked on her little flashlight and began sorting through the beer-can collection that lined the sides of the storm drain. It was Teddy's. Penny sniffed a can, catching the acidy-sweet whiff of long-ago beer. She admired the florid paintings on the sides—the German castles and the huge-breasted women. She had no breasts to speak of herself, unlike Amy. The training bra her mother bought her sagged awkwardly in the front and rubbed the skin under her arms raw. She'd stuck it in the back of her sock drawer, out of sight, preferring to wear cotton undershirts that fit her like a second skin. She didn't need sliding bra straps to remind the boys that she was a girl.

She shifted the cans around and then paused, a shiver running up her spine. Some of the cans were filled to the rim with fresh cigarette butts, and the Old Milwaukee can had been crushed and punctured by something sharp, like a knife. Had someone been down here? The boys didn't smoke, and besides, this was her and Teddy's secret place.

Maybe it wasn't such a good idea to be down in the storm drain now, after dark. Especially since it was so close to Caleb's house, right next to it, really. The storm drain had never been a scary place before, but now her thoughts were racing. What if there was a monster or rats or dead people down here? What if there was something even worse than monsters or dead people? Something that liked to smoke cigarettes and stab cans?

Something like Caleb.

Penny shivered and looked around, terrified now, her imagination racing a million miles a minute. What if Caleb was out there, in the dark night, just waiting to poke out her eye with a hunting knife? She was getting scared, so scared that when she heard a scraping sound at the top of the drain, a sort of shuffling, she just froze.

Someone was right above her. And she could smell cigarette smoke.

She crept backward on her hands and knees to the opening of the storm drain pipe. The woods loomed darkly before her, the moon casting watery shadows through the leafy trees, a breeze stirring restlessly through the hot summer night. She took a deep breath and bolted into the woods.

She had run about a hundred yards when she looked back and saw a shape appear out of the darkness like a wraith. As if sensing her presence, the figure stirred, and then plunged into the woods after her.

Penny didn't think twice. She just ran.

She ran on feet made swift with terror, and with every step she heard something crashing through the brush behind her in the distance. Someone was chasing her. Normally sure-footed, Penny stumbled over plants and tree branches, fear making her clumsy. The woods were so dark she could barely see a step in front of her, the moon now obscured by the thick canopy of trees. She longed to flick on her flashlight but knew that she couldn't—it would give her away.

She abruptly realized that she could scream and no one would ever hear her. What had she been thinking, to run into the woods? she wondered. Wasn't this

Caleb's home turf? Didn't he flush kids like small game into the deep, dark woods and then do terrible things to them?

And then, suddenly, she was falling, her foot caught in a tangle of vines, the flashlight flying from her hand. For a moment she didn't move—the wind was knocked out of her—but then she heard him gaining on her and she was up and off again, her knees wet with fresh blood.

She kept moving, no matter that her knees stung and her stomach was tight with fear. She was the fastest kid on the block, and it was speed alone that was going to get her out of this. She had a bad feeling that he was catching up to her, but she couldn't risk pausing and looking back, and she was thinking that maybe he was going to get her after all when it suddenly appeared out of the darkness—the big, thick old tree, the one wide as a child. *Wide as her.*

Penny slid her slim body behind the tree, flattened herself against it, and went still, the way Mr. Cat did when he was stalking an unsuspecting bird. She closed her eyes and gulped, trying to slow her breathing by sheer force of will. The figure paused as if looking for her and then turned away, disappearing into the shadowy trees.

She exhaled in relief.

A hand grabbed her shoulder. She whirled around, a scream in her throat, blinded by a bright light shining into her eyes.

It was Mac.

"You're It," he said with a grin. And clicked his flashlight off.

CHAPTER 4

The phone calls began at the crack of dawn.

First Mrs. McHale called Penny's mother to say that she had seen Caleb lurking outside the liquor store. Then Mrs. Albright called to say that she had seen a boy who looked suspiciously like Caleb hanging out by the old stone bridge at the bottom of Lark Hill. Finally Mrs. Bukvic called to say that she had heard from another mom that Caleb had been seen clear across town, sitting outside the gas station, at the very same time he was supposed to have been lurking outside the liquor store and hanging out by the Lark Hill bridge. After that, Penny's mother had taken the phone off the hook.

Even so, Penny knew her mother was discomfited by all the calls, because the first words out of her mouth to Teddy and Penny were, "Listen, you two, I don't want you going down to the creek."

Penny's eyes flicked over to Teddy.

"You mean because of Caleb?" Teddy asked nervously.

"No, not because of Caleb," Mrs. Carson said, her mouth twitching. "Why would I say that?"

"That's what the other moms are saying," Penny said, knowing she was pushing the right button.

Even though her mom was friendly with the other mothers, Mrs. Carson made a point of insisting that she had different ideas about how things should be done. And Penny knew that the other mothers sometimes talked about her mom behind her back, saying that she was too liberal.

"Absolutely not. That's all nonsense. I want you to stay away from the creek because there's no one back there to supervise you. You can drown in an inch of water; that's all it takes. Not to mention, there was that boy who got hurt last summer."

"Can we still play in the woods if we promise not to go in the creek?" Penny wheedled.

"Yeah, please, Mom? Otherwise our summer will be *ruined*!" Teddy added with dramatic flair.

Mrs. Carson looked between them and sighed. "I suppose so. As long as you promise to stay away from the creek."

Penny nodded. "We promise."

The swimming hole wasn't the same thing as the creek, exactly.

Penny, wearing her new yellow swimsuit, stood on the edge of the swimming hole trying to decide if she should dive in or just jump.

The water was much lower than usual, and it was dark and slimy because it hadn't rained in weeks. Parts of the creek were dry as a bone. But the swimming hole was the deepest part of the creek, a cozy little bend deep enough to dive into if you were careful. And they were all careful; nobody wanted to end up like Frankie Thomas, the kid from Finch Road who took a dive last summer and hit his head on the bottom. Her father said that he was a real vegetable now, that he couldn't do anything for himself, not even go to the bathroom.

Benji, wearing cutoff jean shorts, took a running leap off the mossy side of the creek, grabbing a rope hanging from the tree. He swung out over the swimming hole like a maniac, hung in midair for a moment, and then, clutching his knees, plunged into the water, hollering, "Cannonball!"

He made an enormous splash.

Heartened, Penny took a deep breath and jumped. She came up, spitting water, to see Mac crouching in the mud, digging at crayfish with a stick. He speared one and waved it about triumphantly.

The trapped crayfish wriggled futilely.

Penny tugged at the seat of her swimsuit. It kept riding up and was giving her a wedgie. She peered into the thick woods, the familiar sound of crickets chirping doing nothing to dispel the fear in her belly. She had told the boys about being followed during flashlight tag, but they dismissed her fears.

"Penny, it wasn't Caleb, it was me," Mac had scoffed.

And while that seemed to make sense, Penny still couldn't shake the feeling that he was wrong, that *somebody else* had been following her the previous night.

Penny paddled around, her feet trailing in the water. She felt a twinge of guilt about disobeying her mother, but it was very hot, and besides, she was a terrific swimmer. The creek was perfectly lovely, better than any old pool, Penny thought.

Was it only two summers ago that she had taken swimming lessons with Amy in the big, deep public pool across town? She remembered how much fun they'd had, how Amy had urged her on whenever she'd been tired or discouraged. She didn't understand why Amy wouldn't play with them now, or why she was so mean to her. Ever since Amy had turned fourteen, she'd been different.

It had happened in the blink of an eye. One day Amy was her friend, and the next day she acted like she didn't even know her. Penny had been so surprised she'd just stared at her, dumbfounded; she'd had the same startled feeling she had when she tripped over her own feet. *How did that happen?*

And so she kept going back to Amy, thinking each time that her friend's behavior had been some sort of freak accident, like a solar eclipse. Except every time from that point on, Amy was mean to her, cruel in a way Penny had seen other girls be to each other. Amy acted as if Penny was some kind of lowlife insect to step on and make fun of. It was like she hated her now.

At a birthday party months ago, Amy had locked Penny in a closet in the basement with a boy who tried to kiss her until she had started crying. The whole time, Penny had heard Amy shrieking with laughter outside the door.

Now Penny's own birthday party was fast approaching, and while she usually looked forward to birthdays, she was feeling some trepidation. She was turning thirteen, an unlucky number if ever there was one. Still, she harbored a secret hope that Amy would be nicer to her once she was thirteen. That everything would be normal again.

"I lost my glasses! I lost my glasses!" Teddy howled.

Teddy had to wear his glasses to swim, and he was always losing them in the water.

Penny sighed. "Where?"

"I don't know!" he said, anxiety rising. "They just fell off!"

"Okay," she said in a calm voice. "I'll find them."

She took a deep breath and dove into the water, swimming hard. She opened her eyes but couldn't see anything; it was too dark and murky. Her fingers touched the silky bottom and she groped around, brushing slimy weeds and something sharp. An aluminum can? Then she needed to breathe, so she struck out for the surface.

"Find them?" Teddy asked hopefully.

She shook her head and, taking another deep breath, dove again. She worked her way gingerly along the bottom and felt something scuttling around. Probably a crayfish. She kept reaching, and then she felt the plastic earpiece of the glasses, tangled in a clump of something, something sort of oval-shaped, she couldn't tell what. She tugged hard but the glasses wouldn't break free, so she reached down with both hands, just ripped the whole clump out, and swam for the surface.

"Found 'em," she called, holding the thing in her hand high. Penny put the clump on the bank and pulled herself out, breathing hard. She rubbed at her eyes, and when she looked up, the boys were staring at her.

"What?"

Teddy was white as a ghost.

Penny looked at the clump, except it wasn't a clump at all. It was a small skull—Teddy's glasses were stuck in the eye socket. Penny stumbled back in horror.

"Looks like a dog," Benji said, kneeling down to inspect the slimy greenish skull.

Oren blanched, and then sighed in relief. "The head's too big for Bozo."

"It was shot," Benji said grimly. "Look." He pointed to a hole in the back of the skull.

"Could've been a hunting accident," Mac said, but even he sounded skeptical.

"I don't think so," Benji said. "It's like a mob execution. *Bam!* Right in the back of the skull."

"Yeah. This would be just like Caleb. What a sicko," Oren said.

"Toby said they were always finding dead animals in the woods back then," Mac said.

"Is it recent?" Penny asked in a hesitant voice, water dripping down her leg.

Benji shrugged. "Hard to say." He fished Teddy's glasses out of the eye socket. "Here."

Teddy took them gingerly and then went down to the water to rinse them off. He slid them on, looked at the kids, and said, "Maybe we shouldn't swim here anymore. There might be more animals in there."

"Or worse," Oren whispered.

Penny looked at the murky water and shivered.

Penny felt like she was going to melt, just like Frosty the Snowman. She was going to turn into a puddle of water, but instead of a carrot and corncob pipe, all they'd find was a batting helmet and Teddy's brand-new Louisville Slugger bat.

It was dusk, the perfect time to play softball. She usually liked being up at bat, but the pressure was on thanks to Zachary, their lame right fielder who had missed every ball hit his way, even the easy fly balls. They had gotten stuck with Zachary because old Mr.

Schuyler, the umpire, thought all kids should play, no matter how fat, or stupid, or just plain inept.

The softball competition was the brainchild of Mr. Schuyler, a retired farmer. He had painted the cul-de-sac with bases and personally supplied batting helmets and balls and bats. Childless themselves, Mr. and Mrs. Schuyler were the block's official grandparents.

The kids competed by streets. The games were held after supper, and all the parents dragged lawn chairs down to the cul-de-sac and watched their kids and gossiped. So, in addition to the pressure of being one run behind and having two men on base and two outs, Penny had the added distraction of the parents gossiping. She kept overhearing snatches of conversation. From what Penny could gather, Amy Bukvic had been seen riding around in a car with some boy. It was widely speculated that this boy was bad news because, as Mrs. Albright declared, he was coming by during the day, when the Bukvics were at work. Penny was very surprised to hear grown-ups discussing kids like this. And then the topic abruptly changed.

One of the mothers asked, in a hushed voice, "Anyone seen Caleb?"

Penny stole a look at the Devlins' house. The driveway was like a car graveyard. There was an ancient

Cadillac on cinder blocks, a rusting Impala, and a Chevy Nova that looked like it had been stripped for parts. There was also a gleaming, new-looking Harley Davidson. No sign of the red Trans Am, though. The blinds were drawn and the porch light turned off. It looked like no one was home.

"Yo, Penny!" Mac shouted.

A ball was coming right at her. She swung too late.

"Stee-rike one!" Mr. Schuyler called.

"Penny, wake up!" Mac hollered.

Penny sighed and hunkered down, trying to pay attention. A lot was riding on her. The winning team was taken to Wallaby Farms for ice cream.

Mrs. McHale said, in a strident voice, "I told Angus that he better not go into those woods."

"I won't let Benji go, either," said Mrs. Albright. "But I have a bad feeling that they go down there anyway. Bud said some lumber at the range is missing. I bet they're building one of their forts."

Penny winced.

And then Mac was shouting and the ball was arcing right past her. Penny forced her arms to move, swinging fast, tipping the ball with her bat. The ball went sailing into the air above Penny, behind home base. The catcher dropped his mask and ran to get under the ball, glove out. The ball landed with a thump in the soft oiled leather and then bounced out, startling the catcher.

"Strike two!" Mr. Schuyler called in a disappointed voice, as if he knew Penny could do better than that. While he was supposed to be an independent umpire, it was well known that he pulled for the Mockingbird Lane kids.

Mac glowered.

Penny made herself stare at the pitcher. The kid spit in his glove, kneaded the ball, and then looked Penny straight in the eye, trying to psych her out.

Kids from the Wren Circle team started shouting, egging her on. *"Hey, batter, batter, batter!"*

"Have you heard from Susie lately?" Mrs. McHale asked in a tentative voice.

"Not a word," Mrs. Albright said. "I'm almost afraid to call her. Wait 'til she finds that they let him out."

"Poor Jeffy. I still can't believe it," Mrs. McHale murmured. "And he was such a nice boy."

Who was Jeffy? Penny wondered. Who was Susie?

The pitcher wound up and threw. She relaxed and swung hard, her bat connecting with the ball. It went flying. She dropped the bat and started to run, but it didn't matter, because the ball had landed on the Bukvics' front lawn. Automatic home run.

"Way to go, Penny!" Mac whooped.

Penny grinned in relief.

Penny was sprawled next to Teddy on the couch in the den, watching television, her belly full of strawberry ice cream, her favorite, when Mrs. Evreth appeared at the door, toting Zachary behind her.

After the game Mr. Schuyler had driven everyone over to Wallaby Farms for ice cream. Well, everyone, that is, except Zachary, who was in the bathroom when they left. It had been hilarious to watch him rushing out of the Albrights' house, running after them as Mr. Schuyler's pickup truck drove away, leaving him in the dust. Mr. Schuyler, who was starting to go deaf, hadn't even heard Zachary's shouts.

Now, watching Zachary stumble forward, his hair matted with blood, tears streaming down his face, a huge bruise on his cheek, Penny was thinking that maybe it hadn't been all that funny.

"Who clobbered you?" Teddy asked in a stunned voice.

This was the wrong thing to say.

"Doctor!" Mrs. Evreth wailed, her thickly coifed curls bobbing frenetically. "Why has God done this to me? I can't believe this. I really can't."

Mrs. Evreth, a divorced single mother, belonged to some strange born-again sect and was always trying to get the kids to come to her "Bible group." Needless to say, none of them ever took her up on her offer, and everyone generally avoided the house at all costs.

"I sent the poor dear to the market for ice cream and some hooligan beat him up," she continued in a rush. "My poor little baby!"

"Little," Penny thought, was not a word that described Zachary Evreth.

Zachary drew a ragged breath. His skin, which looked positively rubbery to begin with, looked even paler in the white light of the kitchen.

"What happened, buddy?" Penny's father asked gently, sitting Zachary down on a chair. Her mother, who was used to people showing up in her kitchen like this, pulled out a box of bandages and medical supplies.

"Go on, Zachary, tell the doctor what that boy did to you," Mrs. Evreth coaxed.

He wore a pained expression. "He punched me like a hundred times right here," he said, tapping his chest. He held out his arm. "And he twisted my arm. It really hurts."

"And he smashed you in the head, too," Teddy added helpfully, pointing at Zachary's blood-matted hair.

"Oh, yeah," Zachary said.

Dr. Carson put his hands on Zachary's chest. "Does this hurt?"

Zachary gave a huff of pain.

"And here?"

A wheeze of discomfort.

Penny's father gently touched Zachary's shoulder, and Zachary yelped.

"Look, Zachary, we're gonna have to take you to the hospital," he said in a deceptively calm voice.

"The hospital!" Mrs. Evreth screeched.

Penny and Teddy exchanged a wide-eyed look.

"It's nothing to worry about, Bernadette," he explained patiently.

"But the hospital!"

"He needs to get an X-ray."

"An X-ray!"

"Yes, an X-ray. He may have a dislocated shoulder, and I want to rule out any broken ribs."

Mrs. Evreth burst into tears. Zachary's lip worked tremulously, as if he, too, was getting ready to cry.

"Bernadette, calm down. Zachary, why don't you

sit here and relax while your mom and I talk for a moment," her father said, steering Mrs. Evreth into the adjoining living room, with Penny's mother following close behind.

Mrs. Evreth's loud voice rang through the house. "Poor Zachary! He doesn't even know how to defend himself. I don't know how he'll survive his teenage years!"

"Now, Bernadette," her father murmured soothingly in his doctor voice.

"And he won't even say who did it!" Mrs. Evreth wailed, her voice rising in pitch. "I just know it was that Caleb Devlin! He's back! I heard from one of the girls in the hair salon!"

Looking at Zachary's pathetic figure, Penny felt a twinge of regret. She knew he wouldn't have gotten beaten up if he'd been with them at Wallaby Farms.

"Uh, you want some ice cream?" Penny offered awkwardly.

Zachary's eyes lit up a fraction. "Sure," he wheezed.

Penny got a bowl, took a carton from the freezer, and scooped out a big chunk of vanilla ice cream. "Sprinkles?" she asked.

He nodded. Penny wasn't surprised. He was a sprinkles kid for sure.

Penny placed the bowl in front of him, and he grabbed the spoon with the hand of his uninjured arm.

"Thanks," he said. His eyes closed in relief as he took a bite of the ice cream.

Penny's eyes met Teddy's for a long moment, and then she asked the obvious. "So, was it Caleb?"

Zachary's mouth screwed up. He took a deep shuddering breath. "It was—"

Penny and Teddy leaned forward to catch his words.

And watched as Zachary tumbled off the chair onto the floor in a dead faint.

Penny had an elaborate series of bedtime rituals.

First she said her prayers. She was very careful to name every member of her family because she knew that if she omitted one, the consequences would be dire. One time she had forgotten to ask God to bless Teddy, and the very next day he had gotten chicken pox.

After the prayers, she lined up the runner on her bedside table so that it was perfectly straight, and turned her pillow so that the open end faced toward the door. The closet had to be shut all the way, because who knew what would come out of it during the night? She knew she was too old for this, but still, the shades had to be pulled down to the ledge, and she positioned her old bear Georgie at the foot of her bed, the first line of defense. It wasn't so much that she feared monsters, but rather an unnamed feeling that if things weren't in the same safe, predictable places when she went to sleep every night, then she was jinxing herself.

And now, with the threat of Caleb heavy in the air, she felt it was especially important for everything to be just right and in its place. Penny painstakingly double-checked her room, taking extra care to make sure that her windows were locked, that the shades were pulled tight, that her flashlight was under her pillow, within easy reach.

"You in bed?" her mother called from the doorway.

Penny scrambled into bed.

Her mother stepped into the room, looking tired and worn-out, a baby spit-up towel over one shoulder. "Ugh," she said, looking down at the floor. "Penny, hand me a tissue. I stepped on a bug."

Penny plucked a tissue from her bedside stand, hoping that if it was a spider it was dead. There was nothing she hated worse than spiders.

"What was it?"

Her mother grimaced. "A ladybug."

From the bed, Penny gasped.

"Penny," her mother said in a weary voice.

"But, Mom!" Penny insisted. "It's bad luck. Really bad luck. Nana says that every time you step on a ladybug, someone dies." *Now she's done it*, Penny thought with a sinking feeling.

Her mom sat down on the bed and smoothed the wispy hair off Penny's forehead with a soothing gesture. "Your Nana is getting superstitious in her old age, and you shouldn't take her so seriously, okay?"

"But—"

"But nothing," her mother said firmly, and switched off the lamp. "You better be asleep by the time your dad gets home."

Just then the front door opened, and Penny heard the heavy footfall of her father.

"Bethany?" he called up the stairs.

"Phil, don't shout. I just put the baby to bed," her mother whispered urgently, and started down the stairs.

Penny slipped out of bed and crept down the hall, pausing outside her parents' room to look in at Baby Sam's crib. He'd managed to throw off his blanket and was fiercely clutching a small pink pig. As if sensing her presence, he snuffled a little, and then settled into soft whispery snoring.

She continued down the dark hall and crouched on the worn carpet on the top stair, listening to the conversation in the kitchen below.

"Want a beer?" her mother murmured.

"More like a dozen," her father said. "What a mess."

"So, is he okay?" her mother asked.

Suddenly Penny felt something brush her leg. She opened her mouth to scream but caught herself. She whirled around.

It was Teddy in his pajamas, hair still wet from his bath. She glared at him.

"What's going on?" he whispered.

Penny held a finger up to her silent lips.

"A sprained shoulder. A couple of stitches. He probably passed out because his mother was carrying on like he was going to die. He'll be okay. But it gave me a scare for a minute, the way he just suddenly keeled over. Reminded me of my residency nights in the ER."

"There was blood all over this kitchen," Penny's mother said.

"You should see the inside of the minivan," her father added ruefully.

Her mother sighed, a sigh that seemed to say that kids bleeding on kitchen floors and on the seats in your minivan were part of the deal when you were married to a doctor.

"Poor kid. Did he say who did it?"

A pause, and then her father said, in a low voice, "When Bernadette asked him if it was Caleb, he started crying."

"But he didn't actually say it was Caleb?" her mother countered.

Her father hedged. "Not in so many words. But he looked like he'd been worked over pretty good by someone."

"Not you, too, Phil," her mother said, her voice thick with disapproval.

Penny looked at Teddy and could see that he was thinking the same thing.

"Phil, don't say it. Don't buy into this small-town hick nonsense," her mother said angrily. Penny and Teddy could hear the sound of dishes being thrown into the sink, water running.

This was so like her mother, Penny thought. Always sticking up for the underdog. As if Caleb could even be remotely considered an underdog!

"I'm sorry," her father said in measured tones. "You

have to see my point, Bethany. Being open-minded doesn't mean we have to be blind to the facts. It *could* have been Caleb."

Penny gasped, startling her brother, who was crouched close behind her. Teddy lost his balance and fell back against the dresser at the top of the stairs, rattling the photos on it. Penny leaped up to steady them.

"Did you hear something upstairs?" her mother asked suspiciously.

"No," her father said, and then murmured something else, something they couldn't hear.

Teddy looked at Penny and gulped fearfully.

Maybe, Penny thought, *it would be a good idea to learn how to shoot that BB gun after all.*

CHAPTER 5

The swimming hole shimmered with the same blue intensity as the sky after a hard rain.

It was a perfect day for a swim. The boys had been silly not to come with her. But she didn't care. She was hot, burning up, her skin prickly with heat rash, and the only thing she wanted to do was float in all that cool water.

Penny perched on the edge, curled her thin body, and then, in one smooth motion, dove into the water, dove deep, deeper than she knew she should have. She opened her eyes, but it was too murky to see; everything was thick and brown as an old shoe. She struck out hard, moved her arms strongly, and broke the surface, gasping for breath. With her eyes still closed, she felt her way to the mossy bank on the other side, hoisted herself up, and crouched there, rubbing furiously at her eyes.

She opened her eyes to a squint and the world wavered in front of her for a moment and then miraculously cleared. That was when she saw the hard black boot in front of her. A cigarette stub fell to the ground, and the boot ground it out. Only then did she look up.

Caleb towered over her, darkly attractive, all hard boy. Her eyes traced the length of his body, noticed the way his legs seemed like whipcords, saw the dirt under his fingernails, the skull tattoo on the back of his hand. He was holding a beer bottle. He took a swig, his head tilting back casually, his thick hair falling in dark waves, like the hair of the Black Knight in her book about King Arthur.

The Black Knight, she thought.

The atmosphere changed abruptly, the sky darkening, the air filling with menace.

Caleb reached out a hand and ran his fingers lightly down her smooth, damp shoulder, raising goose bumps.

She froze, wanting to scream, the hysteria building in her, mounting until all she could do was look on in shock as he brushed a rough finger down her arm. She opened her mouth to scream, but nothing came out; she couldn't make her mouth work.

He smiled at her, his eyes hinting at what he wanted to do, what he could do with stupid little girls like her. He leaned forward, and she felt his breath, pressing, hot on her ear.

"Penny," he whispered huskily.

The bottle of beer fell from his hand, the glass shattering in slow motion, green shards flying through the air.

And then she woke up, breathing hard.

Penny slipped out of the house through the side door in the laundry room while her mother was distracted trying to give the baby a bath. She walked up Mockingbird Lane and took a right down the steep curving slope of Lark Hill Road.

Lark Hill Road was the location of more than one fantastically bloody skateboard wipeout, and was also the best place to go sledding when it snowed. At the very bottom of the hill was a wide old fieldstone bridge, under which the creek flowed. The Lark Hill bridge was a popular place for older kids to smoke and drink beer, usually underneath its wide arches, and empty beer cans spilled out from beneath it.

The woods crowded in on either side of the

bridge. Benji was meeting her here with his BB gun. He was going to teach her how to shoot. There were no homes on Lark Hill Road, and so the bridge was an easy place from which to slip into the woods, because it was out of sight of parents' eyes. Penny's mother would not be happy to see Penny heading into the woods with Benji and his BB gun.

Someone had posted a sign on the bridge wall:

MISSING DOG:
Smoky. Black and white collie mix.
Please call 625-8758 with any information.

Benji biked up a minute later, BB gun in hand.

"Ready?" he asked, chaining his bike to a tree.

They headed deep into the woods, past the fort, where the shots would not be heard by adult ears. The woods were dark and thick, with shafts of sunlight breaking through here and there.

"You getting excited about the Fourth?" Benji asked.

"Yeah," Penny said. "Especially if Mom gets a baby-sitter. I don't want to get stuck watching the dumb baby all day."

As they worked their way through the brush along

the trail, the landscape seemed to change, to turn in on itself, get darker, as if each step away from the bridge was a step farther back in time. The woods had always been a safe place for Penny, a place where nothing bad ever happened, but she found herself looking at it with new eyes, wondering what the mothers meant about Susie and that kid Jeffy.

Penny picked up a long stick, good for walking. "Benji, do you think it's okay that we're back here in the woods? I mean, what about Zachary and all?"

Several days had passed since Zachary had showed up bleeding in the kitchen, and news of his accident had spread like wildfire through the neighborhood. Everybody—kids and adults—was talking about it.

He stiffened slightly and looked at her. Benji was different from the other boys. He was always the first one there when she fell out of a tree, or got the wind knocked out of her during touch football.

"I don't think Caleb really beat Zachary up. Why would he bother? You know how Zachary is," Benji said, his meaning clear. Zachary was just one of those kids who invited bullies. He had years ahead of him filled with black eyes and stolen lunch money.

"But he was a mess," Penny said.

Benji shrugged. "He makes up a lot of stuff. He went hunting with me and the guys this one time. . . ."

Mr. Albright was a big hunter, Penny knew. The Albrights' den had stuffed animal heads mounted on the walls—deer, elk, even a cute little fox.

"This was before his parents got divorced," Benji continued. "Anyway, he wouldn't shoot this rabbit, and his dad yelled at him, and Zachary started crying and stuff, and so Mr. Evreth shot the rabbit. Then he gave it to Zachary, who told everybody he'd killed it. But I'd seen the whole thing."

"I don't know," Penny said. "Caleb *is* back. What if he, you know, put traps back here? Like he did before?"

Benji gave her a cocky look. "That's why I'm teaching you how to shoot, right?"

"Right," she said in a hollow voice.

"Come on, don't worry. I'll look after you," he said, and winked.

They had reached the old springhouse. There was a bull's-eye target pasted to its crumbling side.

"Now this is a real gun, even though it shoots BBs. You can really hurt someone with them, so you have to be careful, okay?" And then he handed her the BB gun reverently.

Penny gripped it gingerly, slightly afraid. "Do you

know some kids named Susie and Jeffy?"

"Kids? From this neighborhood?"

She nodded.

He shrugged. "There was a Jeff, I think, but he was a lot older. Like Toby's age, maybe."

"Oh," Penny said. That was a dead end.

"Why?"

"Nothing." Penny took a deep breath. "How do I hold this thing?"

He positioned the gun in Penny's arms, standing behind her with his hand over hers on the trigger. She could smell the scent of peanut butter rising from his skin, and something else, something distinctly boyish. He steadied her shoulder as she looked down the barrel. His cheek was warm against hers, and she felt a funny tickle in her spine, the same exact feeling she had when she got to the good part of a book.

"Okay?" he asked, twisting slightly to look at her, his eyes dark.

"Yeah," she breathed, fixing her eyes firmly on his. He blinked in surprise and then his lips were hovering over hers, their noses bumping, their lips brushing together, a tantalizing whisper. She stood still for a moment as he moved his lips against hers experimentally, the bubble-gum taste of them, and then, as if suddenly remembering where they were, she pulled away.

Penny hefted the gun and aimed, narrowing her eyes at the target as if that would make her heart stop pounding. The barrel gleamed faintly in the dappled light from the trees. She was thankful she had something to do, to take her mind off what had just happened.

"Where do I look?" she asked shakily.

"Just line up the sights," he instructed, all business now.

She squinted hard, narrowing her eyes.

Benji backed away. "Go for it."

Penny took a deep breath and shot. The gun jumped slightly and bumped against her chin.

"Ow! That hurt," Penny said, rubbing her chin. "Did I hit anything?"

Benji surveyed the bull's-eye. It was perfectly clean.

Penny sighed. This was going to take some time.

"Don't hold it by your chin," he suggested.

"I figured that one out myself, thanks," she said sourly.

Benji said earnestly, "Look, try it again and pretend that there's someone you hate there. You know, like—

I don't know . . . ," he said, his voice trailing off.

Like Caleb, she thought to herself.

She raised the gun and looked down the barrel, and suddenly he was there, as if conjured, glaring at her, taunting her, his eyes dark and cruel, like he couldn't wait to get a piece of her, lure her into the woods and hurt her like he had Zachary Evreth. He pulled a long hunting knife out of the leather case on his belt and caressed the shiny point with one long, greasy finger, running it along the edge of the sharp blade. Without warning he lifted his arm, blade in palm, and threw the knife right at her.

She hissed and fired reflexively.

Benji inspected the target.

"Well?" she asked.

Benji smiled approvingly. "Now you're getting it."

The house was quiet when Penny got home, hot and sweaty from shooting practice.

"Mom?" she called into the warm house. The kitchen felt like a steam bath. Something was definitely wrong with the air conditioner. She wandered around, grabbing a cookie, pouring herself a glass of juice. The note was sitting in the middle of the kitchen table.

Penny loved fresh corn on the cob. Grabbing a clean bowl from a cabinet, another cookie, and her glass of juice, she headed for the garage.

She walked through the laundry room, flicking on lights as she went. Mr. Cat's bowl was full of food, and ants were starting to circle it. He hadn't been home for days now.

The garage was dark and cool, and smelled strongly of gasoline and sawdust. She shucked the corn easily, daydreaming. There was something so soothing about shucking corn. Pulling back piece after piece of crisp green husk to reveal the tender golden corn inside. Penny liked to imagine sometimes that the corn cobs were pretty little dancers and that the husks were their elaborate costumes, their fancy tutus. She pulled a husk down halfway around an ear so that it looked like a girl with a skirt.

"Good evening, ladies and gentlemen," she said, mimicking an emcee. "Welcome to the corn ballet!"

The corn ballerina gave a rousing performance until Penny grew tired of the game and pulled off the husk. She tossed the perfect yellow ear into the bowl with the others.

Penny reached into the sack and pulled out another ear of corn, picking up the cookie with her other hand. She stuffed it whole into her mouth while she methodically ripped off the husks, staring dreamily into space. The corn felt a little squishy and smelled bad, rancid, so she looked down, expecting to see rotten corn. She saw something very different.

A dead rat was cradled perfectly in a spiral of corn husk, with green leaves artfully arranged around its dead body.

Penny started to shake. The rat's eyes were open, the vicious little teeth bared angrily. Its brown-gray fur was soaked with something. She held her fingers up to her face, crumbs falling from her mouth. Her fingers were wet with blood.

She flung the rat away from her, hard. It hit the garage door with a dull thump and slid to the cold cement floor, leaving a bloody mark on the door. Penny fell to her knees, choking on the cookie, coughing it out whole, hysterical, and then she felt that familiar horrible feeling in her chest, the way everything went tight, her stomach churning, her fingers tingling, and she couldn't seem to catch her breath, there was no air and—

"Penny?" a voice said.

She flinched at the sound, whirling around.

"You okay, sweetie?"

Her dad, wearing his lab coat, was standing in the doorway.

That night, after dinner, Penny went looking for Teddy.

She found herself doing this often lately, keeping track of him. She had always been the one to keep an eye on him, but now there seemed even greater reason to make sure her little brother was safe. Especially after what had happened that afternoon.

Her father had stared at the blood-soaked rat for a long time before he said, in a curiously flat voice, "Looks like it just crawled in here to die. They come up when the creek's dry."

"It was *in the corn*, Dad!" Penny had insisted, white-faced and shaking.

"It was probably just hungry, and I'm sure that

corn smelled pretty good."

Still, she couldn't help but remember the way he'd eyed the lock on the garage door, and so she went through the laundry room, opened the door to the garage, and there was Teddy, sitting in the middle of the concrete floor, feeding Tom Ten.

On Mockingbird Lane all the box turtles caught and released were traditionally named Tom. Every once in a while, an empty shell would turn up in the woods with a painted number denoting which Tom it had been.

Teddy was hand-feeding the turtle little bits of lettuce. Tom Ten had been quite snappish when they'd first brought him home and put him in his new cardboard box with some grass. But as the days went by, he had grown bolder, and he would now eat out of Teddy's hand and raise his head when someone came into the dank room. They'd had him for a while, and Penny was starting to think that maybe it was time to let him go. She knew that the longer you kept a turtle, the better chance it had of dying. Also, she was pretty sure that the fumes from the cars were not good for it.

"He's really hungry tonight," Teddy said enthusiastically.

"Yeah?" Penny asked, peering into the cardboard

box. It was seriously smelly. Tom Ten pooped a lot for a turtle, and the grass in the box was getting kind of putrid. "Here, let's take him out."

She reached in, picked up Tom Ten easily, and carried him out of the garage onto the front lawn. It was dark, but everybody had turned on their front lights. She placed him on the fresh-cut grass and his head lunged out of the shell, tasting freedom.

"I think we should maybe let him go," Penny said in a gentle voice.

"Let him go?" Teddy asked with a whine.

"Look at him. He's sick of living in that stinky box. Remember what happened to Tom Nine?"

Benji, like Penny and Teddy, had kept Tom Nine in his garage. After several months of captivity, the turtle had somehow managed to overturn the box and had almost escaped when Benji's dad backed over him in his Oldsmobile, smashing the turtle like a pancake.

Teddy's face fell. "I guess so. But can I be the one to let him go?"

Tom Ten was already booking away from them in the grass.

"Sure," Penny said. "Let's do it in the backyard."

Teddy grabbed up Tom Ten and they went around to the back, with Penny switching on the outside lights as they walked.

When they reached the back lawn, Teddy put the turtle down. Tom Ten looked around, as if taking stock of his new environment, and then trucked away at a steady pace, heading deep into the dark woods.

"You think he'll be okay in the woods?" Teddy asked, a little anxiously.

"Sure, he's got a real hard shell," she said, watching the painted number 10 glow faintly in the dark as the turtle moved through the grass.

Penny looked deep into the dark woods and secretly wondered if Tom Ten would be all right, or if by some horrible freak chance Caleb was back there in the thicket, just waiting to make turtle soup. She didn't want to think about that.

"Look," Teddy said, pointing to the night sky. "A shooting star."

"Nah," Penny said. "It's probably just an alien."

He looked at her and giggled.

They sat there on the patio and watched Tom Ten make his long journey until their mother called them in.

CHAPTER 6

Mac had come up with a plan to make some fast cash to buy fireworks for the Fourth of July.

"I really want to get Roman candles," he said. "I know a guy I can buy them from."

The parents refused to have anything more exciting than sparklers, insisting that the fireworks organized by the local fire department at a nearby park were perfectly adequate. But Mac, who had never been one to let grown-ups get in the way of his grand schemes, had been stockpiling fireworks forever—firecrackers, smoke bombs, bottle rockets—all purchased illegally. He kept his secret stash in a battered steel box tucked into the hollow of a tree. The tree itself was deep in the woods, far past the fort, situated on the edge of a high, treacherous cliff that overlooked the creek far below, so that even the most suspicious father wouldn't find it if he decided to check out their fort. The boys also stored their BB guns in the tree.

"We've got all these kids here every night for softball," Mac had said. "Let's have a haunted house and make 'em pay to go through."

"We can do it at my house," Benji suggested.

However, Mrs. Albright had no intention of letting every kid in the neighborhood tromp through her house. "You can do it in the backyard," she said firmly.

And so the haunted house idea was amended to a "haunted trail," to be held the evening before Penny's birthday party.

The kids set up the trail over two long days. Benji conned his dad into letting them borrow slabs of slate intended for a garden path, which they planted in the ground, like tombstones, and inscribed with chalk epitaphs such as "Rest in Pieces" and "Here Lies Skel E. Ton." A rubber hand in the dirt in front of one of the tombstones gave the effect of a corpse clawing its way out of a grave. Mac planned to supply scary music—groans and moans and clanking—piped in from his older brother's speakers. Oren painted Ping-Pong balls to look like eyeballs, for pelting at kids as they went through, and Penny made fake blood from corn syrup and red food coloring.

They decided to charge fifty cents to go through, and to sell refreshments as well. The mothers were happy to help out, as they were under the impression that the kids were trying to raise money for new softball equipment. Penny's mom made chocolate chip cookies, Mrs. Albright supplied festive little bags of popcorn, and Mrs. McHale baked a batch of oatmeal cookies.

Mrs. Loew contributed a bag of store-bought cookies, which the boys thought was lame; but Penny, who had overheard her mother talking on the phone with Oren's mom, whispering about a divorce, figured that Mrs. Loew had better things to worry about than baking cookies. ·

"I certainly hope you kids aren't driving Mrs. Albright crazy," Mrs. Carson said as Penny and Teddy dug through the oversized hanging plastic garment bags where Halloween costumes and old clothes were stored.

Boxes and old junk were piled in the middle of the attic, where long strips of plywood flooring had been nailed down. Pink cotton-candy insulation extended beyond the flooring on all sides. Teddy stood at the edge of the flooring on the far side of the attic, looking like he wanted to take a leap onto the fuzzy stuff.

"Teddy, get away from that insulation!" his mother ordered.

"Why?" he asked mutinously.

"Because it's very dangerous. There's bits of sharp glass in all that pink fuzz."

He peered down at it as if he didn't quite believe her.

Penny was trying on a red yarn wig, the remnant of an old costume. She modeled the wig with a little shake of her head.

"You look stupid!" Teddy said.

"What was this from, Mom?" Penny asked, her hair sticking out from underneath the yarn.

"A costume party Dad and I went to before we got married. I was Raggedy Andy and your dad was Raggedy Ann."

"Raggedy Ann? No way," Teddy moaned. "Dad wouldn't dress like a girl!"

"Trust me, your dad made a very cute Raggedy Ann," Mrs. Carson said wryly.

Penny and Teddy burst out laughing.

"You kids would tell me, you know, if anyone was giving you a hard time, right?" her mother asked abruptly.

Penny thought of the dog skull at the creek. She

couldn't tell her mother about that because she wasn't supposed to be down at the creek. And she couldn't really confess her fears about Caleb because her mother didn't like them to talk about him. When it came right down to it, there really wasn't *anything* she could tell her.

Finally Penny said, "Like a strange man asking us to take a ride or something?"

"Exactly," her mother answered.

There was a moment of silence as Penny looked past her mother at Teddy, who was sitting very still.

"Sure, Mom," she said, but she wouldn't meet her eyes.

Bats flying crazily above the Albrights' house lent a scary cast to the night of the Mockingbird Lane Haunted Trail. The Albrights' backyard looked downright forbidding in the dark. It was perfect.

Penny, wearing a sheet and a rubber skull mask, was more excited about the haunted trail than her birthday, which was the next day. All the kids would be coming over for her party the next evening—everyone except Zachary, of course—and she was a little worried. She had invited Amy, and she was starting to think that maybe it hadn't been such a good idea. How did you go from being someone's best friend to not existing?

She was stationed with Oren behind the barbecue pit, which bordered on the woods. Her job was to throw fake guts at the kids as they passed. She'd taken a bucket, put cherry Jell-O, rubber snakes and worms, and plastic spiders into it, and mixed it all up.

"It looks pretty real," Oren said approvingly.

"Hey, I know how we can make it look even cooler," Mac said. He pulled out his Swiss Army knife and grabbed Penny's hand, holding it over the bucket and pressing the knife edge against her palm.

"No!" Penny shouted, going white.

Oren shoved Mac away. "Knock it off!" He turned to Penny, who was shaking. "You okay?"

"You're such a jerk," Penny snarled at Mac.

Mac rolled his eyes. "Duh, I was just kidding."

"It's not funny," Oren said. "You know she has a thing—"

"Yeah, yeah, whatever," Mac said, and sauntered off, snickering.

Oren and Penny were looking at each other in disbelief when they heard a voice say "Ow!" Zachary appeared with his arm in a sling.

"Mac just punched me in my bad shoulder," Zachary whined, eyes watery. He was rubbing his shoulder gingerly with his good arm. The bruise on his cheek was a yellowing purple blotch and his hair was pushed back off his forehead, revealing his stitches.

"Hi, Zachary," Penny said unenthusiastically.

Mac wandered back, carrying a bag full of rubber snakes and spiders. "We're not open yet, lame brain."

Zachary looked at Penny. "I can help," he offered in a hopeful voice.

"I'm sure," Mac said derisively.

Penny felt bad. "You could take the money," she suggested. She looked at the other boys. "We need someone to take the money."

"No way," Mac said swiftly.

Oren's face brightened. "Wait a minute, Zachary." He walked away from Zachary and waved the other kids to him. "We'll get a ton more kids to go through the trail if we have Zachary. I mean, we'll get kids who'll come just to *see* him!"

"Oren's right," Penny agreed. "He's practically famous since he got beat up by Caleb."

"Whatever." Mac shrugged.

The kids walked back to Zachary, who was waiting patiently.

"Sure, Zach. You take the money," Benji said.

"Don't even think of stealing any," Mac growled.

Zachary grinned. "I won't."

The first kids Mac brought through were from Wren Circle, and the littlest one was so scared that he burst into tears when Penny threw the guts at him. Penny had to take off her mask and turn on her flashlight to prove that it was just a bucket of cherry Jell-O with a few plastic spiders and rubber snakes, and not real guts. After that, Penny only pelted the older kids.

Toward the end of the night, Penny had to go to the bathroom, but her hands were too gooey for her to go inside, so she snuck into the woods and hid behind a tree. As she crouched there, she heard a rustle, but it was dark under the cover of the trees, so dark that she couldn't see anything.

"Who's there?" she called softly. "Is that you, Oren?"

Silence, and then the crunch of a footstep.

"You can't come back here. I'm going to the bathroom."

Another crunch, closer this time.

"I mean it, you guys. Don't be jerks."

She hastily wiped herself with a few leaves,

dragged up her shorts, and flicked on her flashlight in the direction of the crunch, but nothing was there. Just shadows.

Penny ran back up the slope.

"Can't you guys leave me alone for five minutes?" she said.

"What are you talking about?" Mac asked.

They were all there: Benji, Mac, Oren, and Teddy.

"I was just going to the bathroom, back there in the woods behind the pit, and I heard one of you guys walking around."

"It wasn't us, Penny," Teddy said, looking perplexed.

"Yeah, we've been here the whole time," Oren chimed in.

"Well, if it wasn't any of you, then who was it?" Penny asked, getting scared.

"It was probably just a deer or some other animal," Mac scoffed. "Why are you being such a scaredy-cat, Penny? There's nothing back there but trees."

"Yeah, but—"

"C'mon Penny, the kids are coming!" Oren cried, waving for her to duck down, out of sight.

She pulled the bucket close to her on the ground and put her hand into the guts, waiting for the perfect moment to fling some at the approaching kids. She could hear them coming, not far away, and then she felt it. Something sort of soft and round. She rolled it back and forth in her hand. It was the size of a small Super Ball, but it was softer, mushier. What the heck? She flicked on her flashlight and shone it into the bucket.

Balanced between her thumb and forefinger was a perfect eyeball.

A real one.

It fell from her fingers and the flashlight in her hand shook, the light streaking back and forth, revealing the grisly contents of the bucket, like something right out of a horror movie.

A length of intestine, a glistening pink tongue, and a soft, furry ear, like a small dog's.

Penny felt the horror race up her spine, and then, as if from a very great distance, as if it was happening to someone else, she felt her lungs freeze up, felt her breath strain to come through the hot rubber mask.

"*Pssst!* Penny! Are you asleep back there?" Oren called to her.

But Penny was frozen; she couldn't move.

"Penny?" Oren whispered, concerned, clicking on his flashlight and pointing the beam at her. "Penny!" he yelled, running over to her and ripping off her mask.

Penny's face was white, and she was hyperventilating.

"Oh, man!" Oren yelled, dragging Penny behind him to the deck and the lights, the bucket forgotten. "Get a paper bag! Get a paper bag!"

Benji took off for the house at a tear, and soon Penny was surrounded by all the boys.

"Penny, slow down, breathe," Oren said, his face strained with worry.

This had happened before. The boys knew the drill. "Slow down," they all said.

But she couldn't seem to catch her breath. The harder she tried, the harder it was to get any air in; she opened and closed her mouth like a beached fish.

"Hold on, Penny, here comes Benji," Oren said, patting her back.

And then blessed relief as the paper bag was opened over her face and her lungs took over; they knew what to do. Benji and the magic paper bag. *My hero,* she thought over and over.

Mr. and Mrs. Albright came running out of the house.

"Penny, honey, are you okay?" Mrs. Albright asked, smoothing the hair back from Penny's forehead in a motherly fashion.

Penny nodded her head weakly. She felt dizzy.

"What happened back here?" Mr. Albright demanded furiously, his cheeks red. "Boys?"

Mr. Albright could be a scary guy when he wanted to. He was big and heavy, and got right up into your face, and he had no qualms about shouting at kids, even if they weren't his.

Benji threw up his arms in confusion. "Penny just started to, you know, wheeze, probably because of it being so hot under the mask and all."

"Penny," Mr. Albright asked, clearly suspicious of his son, "is that what happened?'

"Yes, sir," she squeaked. But Penny knew it wasn't the mask that had made her stop breathing. It was fear—the tight, clawing sensation of panic.

"Well, then. That's enough of your haunted trail for one night. You kids get your stuff and go on home. It's nearly ten thirty, anyway," he said sternly.

"Sure, Dad," Benji said obediently. "I'll be right in."

The boys circled Penny, who was seated at the picnic table.

Zachary came around the side of the house, carrying the coffee can full of money. "I've still got kids waiting to go through," he said.

"Tell them to go home," Benji said firmly.

"The bucket," Penny said, sounding as if she was about to cry.

"What's going on?" Zachary asked eagerly.

"What about the bucket?" Benji demanded.

"It's full of guts and—"

"No kidding, Penny, that's what you put in the bucket!" Mac said sarcastically.

Benji whirled on Mac, brandishing a fist: "Shut up so she can talk." He turned back to Penny. "What do you mean?"

"Guts," she said, and then corrected herself. "*Real* guts."

The boys went over to the barbecue pit and gathered around the bucket. Benji shone his light into it. Mac gestured toward where Penny was sitting. He pointed a finger at his head and twirled it. Crazy.

Benji and Oren nodded. Teddy bit his lip, a worried expression on his face.

"You guys see it?" Penny called.

Mac hoisted the bucket and brought it over to Penny. She jumped up and fell back, knocking over the bucket. The contents spilled out on the well-lit cedar deck Mr. Albright had just built a month before.

It was just Jell-O and toys.

"I saw it!" she said in a shaking voice. "It was there! There was an eye, and an ear. Like from a dog!"

"An ear?" Oren asked doubtfully.

"I saw it! Somebody must have switched it or something! Caleb did it!" she cried wildly.

Zachary looked around uneasily.

Teddy grabbed his sister's hand. "C'mon Penny, let's go home. It's late."

"But I saw it," she said brokenly, starting to cry.

"Go home, Penny," Benji said in a gentle voice.

Teddy tugged Penny past the curious kids still lined up waiting to go through the trail.

"Hey! Wait up, you guys!" Zachary shouted, catching up to Penny and Teddy.

The three of them walked in uncomfortable silence up the block.

"I gave the money to Mac," Zachary said, trying to make conversation. He dug around in his pockets and pulled out a mangled-looking piece of bubble gum. "Want a piece?"

"No, thanks," Penny said glumly. She couldn't get the image out of her mind—the guts in the bucket, everything so red and slimy.

"I believe you," Zachary said earnestly.

She stopped in mid stride.

"You do?" she asked, turning to him, taking in his sweaty forehead, the way his jeans were too tight across his belly. "Really?"

"Yeah," he said, slightly raising his arm in its sling.

Penny looked down the block at the Albrights' house, a dejected expression on her face. "I wish the guys did."

"It's okay," Zachary said.

Penny turned to him and said, spontaneously, "Want to come to my birthday party tomorrow night?"

He smiled tremulously.

"Sure," he said.

CHAPTER 7

S he could hardly believe it.

There were no pancakes.

Her mother always made her pancakes on her birthday, sometimes blueberry ones, and once even chocolate chip. But this morning, the only thing waiting for her was cold cereal, a barfing baby brother, and a harried-looking mother. There was not a pancake in sight.

Penny was very superstitious about birthdays. Your birthday predicted what the rest of your year would be like. A bad birthday meant a bad year. Which is exactly what had happened last year. She'd accidentally killed a cricket on her birthday and the whole year had been one big disaster. Amy had been mean to her at every opportunity, she'd gotten a little brother instead of a little sister like she'd hoped, and a case of the chicken pox had prevented her from trying out for softball. Not to mention that her hamster had run away, and she had a sneaking suspicion that Mr. Cat had eaten it. Twelve had been a bad year. She was fervently hoping thirteen would be better, but the lack of pancakes seemed like a bad omen.

She stepped out the front door, and there was Mrs. Bukvic, wearing a suit and looking around anxiously.

"Buster!" Mrs. Bukvic called out in a syrupy voice. "Come home to Mommy!"

The boys were already hard at work by the time Penny got down to the woods. The construction of the fort was coming along fine. Mac had filched a big strip of scrap carpet, which they were using to cover the plywood floor; Benji had cleverly nailed on steps made out of bits of the two-by-fours; and Oren had built an ingenious hidden cabinet where they stored their tools and comic books.

"Hey, Penny," Benji said, a wary expression on his face, like he was worried that she might break or something. "Happy birthday!"

"Thanks," she said, forcing herself to grin at him like everything was just great, like she didn't feel shaky and out of sorts because of the lack of pancakes. She shook her head and stared off into the distance. That was when she saw it.

"You guys!" she called. "Check this out!"

The boys walked over to Penny, and she pointed to the tree. Someone had carved a ragged lightning bolt about two inches long into the bark.

"Looks like a trail blaze," Oren said. "We learned about those last year in Scouts."

Oren *would* know something like this; he was a human encyclopedia.

"Yeah, I remember," Benji said. "You carve them on trees or make little markings with, like, sticks and rocks and stuff."

"What are they for?" she asked.

"They're for when you're lost, so people can find you," Oren said.

"Or as warnings," Benji added. "Looks fresh. You remember what this one means?"

Oren seemed to think for a moment, his eyes scrunched hard in concentration, and then he abruptly went pale. He looked at them helplessly. "I think it means danger," he said in a shaky voice.

"Danger?" Mac demanded. "Is he right?" Mac would rather die than be in anything lame like the Boy Scouts.

Benji nodded. "Yeah, now I remember. It marks

dangerous spots, like bear dens and stuff."

"There aren't any bears in these woods," Teddy said firmly, and then wavered. "Right?"

"I knew we shouldn't have built the fort here," Penny finally whispered. "This is a bad place."

"Can it with the superstitious stuff, Penny," Mac said.

"But Caleb must have carved this into the tree. It's a warning to stay away!"

"No way," Mac said.

"C'mon, Mac, what if—"

"No way!" Mac said. "We just finished building this fort. We are not walking away because we're scared of what he *might* do." His face was red with anger.

When Mac got this way, there was no talking to him. Penny stalked away, down toward the dry creek bed. She had her bathing suit on and needed to cool off, needed to get away from stupid, stubborn boys. She would go to the swimming hole and take a dip. It made her so mad sometimes, how they wouldn't listen to her, just because she was a girl.

She was winding her way along the creek when suddenly something caught her eye. There, farther down the creek, on a rocky ledge, was a flash of orange. It looked like Mr. Cat. He was just lying there, his eyes glittering brightly in the distance. So this was where he'd been.

"Mr. Cat!" she called. "Here, kitty!"

The cat didn't move. She loved Mr. Cat, but honestly, he was so stupid, the way he was always running away all the time.

"Come on, Mr. Cat! Time to go home."

She had nearly reached the cat when she knew something was wrong. No living animal should be that still, that motionless.

"Mr. Cat!"

The cat was frozen in an attack crouch, his claws out, his fur stiff and flecked with blood. His eyes glittered unnaturally, glassy and bright red. A red so bright they seemed to glow.

Someone had killed Mr. Cat.

And stuffed him.

Penny let out a warbled scream and started to back away from the cat, her throat gasping, and then she was running along the dry creek bed, stumbling over the smooth stones, the fetid little pools of water.

She was out of breath and wild-eyed when she reached the fort. The boys stopped what they were doing, taking in her scared expression.

"Somebody killed Mr. Cat!"

They all just stared at her.

Teddy asked, in a trembling voice, "Somebody killed Mr. Cat?"

"Yes!" she shouted. "And they stuffed him!"

They dropped their tools and took off after her, back along the creek bed. Penny stopped abruptly, about twenty feet from the ledge. She pointed.

"Over there."

The boys walked over to the ledge.

Penny crouched on the dry creek bed, clutching her knees and rocking back and forth, her mind whirling. She knew Caleb had done it, knew at the bottom of her soul that he was the one, he'd always had a thing for killing animals. It was his trademark.

"There's nothing here!" Mac called.

"What?" she asked, standing up and jogging over to where they were standing.

Benji shook his head at her, a disappointed look on his face.

Penny's eyes widened. The ledge was bare!

"But Mr. Cat was right there!"

"Maybe Mr. Cat was there, but he was alive, and when he heard us coming, he ran off," Teddy suggested.

"No way. Mr. Cat was dead. Stuffed. And his eyes were weird. They were, like, all red," Penny said.

Oren went still, his eyes narrowing slightly.

"Red, huh?" Mac asked in a sarcastic tone.

Benji nosed around the ledge. "Check this out," he said.

There was a pile of cigarette butts and an empty, crumpled cigarette packet.

"See!" Penny hissed. "That's proof! Caleb was here, and he killed my cat."

Mac slapped his head in mock disbelief. "I mean, c'mon, lots of kids smoke," he said. Then he paused. "Even I do, sometimes."

"You smoke?" Benji asked suspiciously. "No way."

Mac shrugged. "Sure."

Oren weighed in. "Mac's right. It's not proof."

"It was Caleb! He's after me, I know it," Penny said with conviction.

"Whatever, Penny," Mac said, dismissing her. "First the rat, and then the guts, and now this?"

Penny shook her head wordlessly. They didn't believe her!

"C'mon, you guys," Mac said, walking away.

Benji sighed sadly and followed Mac. "See you at the party later," he called out to Penny consolingly.

That was when she knew her year was pretty much ruined.

The next morning, Penny stood in the driveway, admiring her new pink bike. Her birthday party had been a success, with the exception of Becky Albright bursting into tears when she was told that there were no presents for her to open. All the neighborhood kids had come except one. Amy Bukvic.

Penny glanced across the street, and as if it knew Penny was thinking about Amy, the Bukvics' front door opened. Amy walked out carrying a present and wearing a mulish expression on her face, obviously being forced by her mother to go over.

"Here," Amy said, thrusting the package at Penny. "It's a T-shirt."

"Uh, thanks," Penny said warily.

Amy had done something to her hair. It was tinted like a grown-up's, with thin streaks. *She looks so much older than me*, Penny suddenly realized.

"Nice bike," Amy said, all false smiles.

Penny went pale, utterly devastated. It was obvious to her that Amy thought the bike was stupid. "Yeah?" she said weakly.

"Yeah. It looks just like a little-girl bike," Amy

observed, and then shrugged. "Which makes sense, I guess."

"I'm thirteen now," Penny said, swallowing hard.

Amy swept her eyes up and down Penny's gangly body, her tone mocking. "Really?"

"Yes," Penny whispered. "Why are you doing this?"

"Doing what?"

"You know, being like this," Penny said, struggling not to cry.

"I don't know what you're talking about." A pause. "Oh, by the way, Stu said any time you want to make out in a closet again, just let him know," she said, and winked.

And then she turned and walked away.

It was nearly bedtime, and Penny and Teddy were in the den trying to squeeze in every last minute of television when the front door opened and Mrs. Bukvic called out, "Bethany?"

"In the dining room, Betty Ann," her mother called back.

"What are you doing?" Mrs. Bukvic asked.

"Icing about a hundred cupcakes for the Fourth of July party," her mother said.

"Now?" There was censure in Mrs. Bukvic's voice.

"Won't the icing go bad?"

"I'll freeze 'em. The kids won't care. They'll still taste good. What's up?" her mother asked, a little wearily. Penny knew Mrs. Bukvic sometimes got on her mom's nerves, and part of her wondered if it was because of how mean Amy was to her.

"I tell you, those people have no manners. Why, he pushed me off his front step! Can you even believe it?" Mrs. Bukvic exclaimed.

"What people?"

"Ralph Devlin. The man's crass as a cow," Mrs. Bukvic said.

Penny could almost hear her mother sigh.

"And let me tell you, their bushes could stand to be pruned. Not to mention the fact that their geraniums looked positively ill. You'd never catch *my* geraniums looking like that."

Penny's mother said gently, "Ruthie is very sick, Betty Ann. Why did you go down there, anyway?"

"Because of Buster, of course!"

"Buster?" her mother asked, confused.

"Buster's missing, Bethany! I let him out in the backyard, and now he's gone. I just know Caleb took him!"

Penny paled. Buster was gone, too? She thought

about Mr. Cat, and a tight feeling rose in her throat.

"Betty Ann," her mother said in a warning voice.

"So I went down there to see for myself," Mrs. Bukvic continued righteously. "Anyway, all I asked him was whether or not Caleb was back in town, because I could see someone in the kitchen smoking a cigarette. And then Ralph Devlin started yelling at me, and pushed me off his front step!" She added indignantly, "Can you believe the gall of that man?"

"I see," her mother murmured.

"Don't look at me like that! It's my civic duty to stay informed! Caleb is a menace. I'm going to call the police first thing in the morning and demand that they search that house for Buster!"

"You know, Betty Ann, I happen to think that even if Caleb's back, it's not a problem. The kid's what, seventeen? He's practically grown up. I can't imagine why he'd bother with our kids. Or your dog," she added.

"You just don't know," Mrs. Bukvic said darkly. "You don't know what it was like before you got here."

"But how bad could he have been, anyway? He was just a kid then. I think you all make him out to be something worse than he possibly could have been, like a bogeyman or something."

"I'm telling you, he was bad news. He used to catch stray cats and skin them. He put a live rat in the Loews' mailbox. He carried around this great big hunting knife. He did sick things, Bethany, things no child should ever do. Why, he even frightened me, a grown woman!"

"Betty Ann!"

"He killed his own sister," Mrs. Bukvic whispered conspiratorially.

"Oh, please."

"He did!"

Penny glanced at Teddy, and he shook his head in bewilderment.

"I heard that Caleb didn't like the boy she was going out with, so he cut the brakes on the kid's car. His sister wasn't supposed to be in the car when it crashed, just the boy."

"You told me before that was never proven," her mother said.

"Well, no, the car was too badly damaged in the fire, but I remember him threatening that boy because he didn't want his sister going out with him," Betty Ann retorted.

"That's like a bad TV movie," her mom said with a laugh. "Something someone made up."

"Well, nobody made up Jeffy Winegarten in a coma!"

"Who?" her mother asked in a startled voice.

"Jeffy Winegarten. It happened before you moved here. He was the reason Caleb was sent away."

Penny pricked up her ears.

"Caleb put Jeffy into a coma. He tried to beat him to death with a rock."

Her mother made a protesting sort of sound, but Mrs. Bukvic barreled on.

"And that wasn't even the worst of it. Why, he tortured that boy! Both his hands were broken!" Mrs. Bukvic said.

"What?" her mother asked, with a sharp intake of breath.

"Caleb made up some lie that Jeffy fell down a cliff at the creek or some nonsense, but the real story is that Caleb caught Jeffy stealing from his fort. Anyway, Jeffy never came out of the coma. Susie Winegarten's family was from Kansas, so they took Jeffy and moved back there. Janine still talks to her sometimes."

"But it could have been an accident, like Caleb said."

"Bethany, *all* of Jeffy's fingers were broken. That is just not something that happens by accident."

"I still can't imagine a young boy doing that," her mother said, sounding shaky even to Penny's ears.

Mrs. Bukvic had to get the last word in.

"You weren't here when he was growing up. You'll never get it," she insisted loudly.

But Penny, who was listening to every word, did get it.

CHAPTER 8

When Penny first smelled the smoke, she thought she was imagining things.

It was late afternoon the following day, and they were at the fort, hanging out.

That morning, Penny had gone back to look at the missing-dog sign by the bridge. It had been joined by one for Buster, as well as one for a missing Dalmatian up on Cardinal Drive. She wanted to tell the boys about the missing pets, but after the incident in the woods with Mr. Cat, they weren't listening to her. Only Zachary believed her, but he didn't really count.

Besides, there were problems more pressing than Caleb to occupy them now. Dr. Loew had moved out of the family house and into an apartment.

Oren sat in the corner of the fort, looking like he'd been hit with a Mack truck.

"Uh, want part of my candy bar?" Teddy asked him, breaking off a melting piece of chocolate.

As if on autopilot, Oren took the candy, put it into his mouth, and began to chew.

"Hey, Oren!" Benji said with exaggerated enthusiasm. "I say we rig up one of your remote-control cars and strap on some firecrackers and drive it around the block and set them off. We can hide in the bushes by the Schuylers' and watch it all! Wouldn't that be cool?"

Oren shrugged noncommittally, looking down at his chocolaty fingers.

And that was when Penny smelled the smoke, an acrid odor in the air.

"You guys smell that?" she asked, wrinkling her nose.

Benji stood up, stretching slightly, his head hitting the roof. "Yeah."

"Where's it coming from?" Penny asked, a bad feeling crawling up her spine.

"Maybe a barbecue," Teddy suggested.

"Smells more like burning leaves," Mac said with a knowing sniff.

"Who'd be burning leaves this time of year?" Oren asked. "My dad always burns leaves in the fall."

His voice trailed off, as if it suddenly occurred to him that his dad might not be around to burn any leaves this fall.

Black smoke drifted in through a window.

"What the——?" Mac asked.

The crackling of burning wood and dry twigs suddenly seemed loud, and close. The wind shifted abruptly, washing in a cloud of smoke that billowed in black waves.

"I think . . . ," Teddy said shakily. "I think it's a fire."

Penny leaned to look out the window on the other side and felt her heart pound painfully.

"The fort's on fire!"

The boys shoved Penny out of the way, looking down at the rising flames that flickered around the trees supporting the fort. The boards that they'd nailed on to serve as steps were burning brightly, the cheap, dry wood catching fire easily, like kindling.

"What do we do?" Teddy demanded fearfully.

Mac took charge. "Everyone on the roof. Penny, you go first."

Penny didn't argue, she just stepped out the door, grabbed a tree branch, and started to climb, Benji one breath behind her. As Penny nimbly scaled the tree, she saw that the woods surrounding the fort were ablaze.

And then they were all on the roof, clutching tree limbs.

"Now what?" Penny asked. "We can't stay up here."

"We could jump," Benji said.

"No way!" Oren said. "We'll die if we jump."

"We'll slide down this tree," Mac said, gripping a slender bark-encrusted tree that grew parallel to the trees supporting the fort. It was a young, green tree, and on fire, but not as badly as the other ones.

"How?" Benji asked. "We'll burn off our hands."

"I got it figured out. Everyone take off your shirts," Mac ordered.

The boys quickly stripped their shirts over their heads, revealing tan bellies. After a moment, Penny did too, grateful that she was wearing an undershirt, even if it was a pink one with little yellow roses. Imagine her embarrassment if she'd actually been wearing that awful training bra! As it was, Benji cast a surreptitious glance at the undershirt.

"Follow me," Mac declared, and, reaching out, wound his T-shirt around the tree and started to slip down the tree with the shirt, the fabric slowing his slide and blotting out the flames. He reached the bottom and waved. Benji and Oren were down in short order. Teddy looked tremulously at Penny.

"You go first," she said.

He bit his lip. "But you're a girl. I should go last."

"Just go," Penny ordered, starting to cough from the smoke.

"Hurry!" Benji shouted from the ground.

With a last look, Teddy slid down, and then, confident he was safe, Penny reached out for the tree, wrapped her T-shirt around it, and started the perilous trip down. She was halfway down when she heard the crack.

The next thing she knew, she was falling, tumbling through the air. She fell into a tangle of leaves and branches on the ground, her rear end slamming the dirt and her wrist bending awkwardly under the impact. The boys were around her in a heartbeat, urging her up, the flames close now.

"You okay?" Benji shouted through the smoke, an arm around her waist. "The tree broke!"

"No kidding," she said, wincing.

For a moment the kids looked up at the fort, mouths open, watching all their hard work go up in flames. The wind blew and a wave of black smoke wafted over them, and when Penny's eyes cleared, she saw Benji looking the other way.

"Oh no," Benji whispered.

They turned and saw the fire roaring up the slope toward the houses.

"It's heading for *my* house!" Mac shouted.

They tried to run around the fire toward the McHales' house, but the smoke was suffocating and they couldn't find a clear path. Coughing for air, their eyes stinging, they knew they'd never make it if they went that way.

"Turn around," Mac called.

They doubled back, the flames behind them now, at their shirtless backs, heating their bare skin, the horrible crackle of igniting trees sharp in their ears. Mac led them down to the creek, and they scrambled as fast as they could over the dry rocky bed. Penny clambered after the boys up the bank by the Lark Hill bridge, and then started the trek up Lark Hill Road. She was tired, and her throat hurt from the smoke, and her wrist was throbbing.

They were halfway up the hill when the police car and fire engines went screaming past, and by the time they made it down the block, the engines were already parked in front of the McHales' house. Huge firemen carried impossibly long hoses into the backyard. All the moms were huddled together on the sidewalk by the house, whispering and consoling Mrs. McHale, who was beside herself. When she saw Mac, she broke free of the women and ran to him.

"What were you doing in the woods?" she cried angrily, and then pulled him into her arms, hugging him hard.

He didn't bother to deny it. "Lemme go," he said.

Mrs. Albright rushed forward to grab Benji, her face tear-stained. "And you, young man, are in serious trouble. You are grounded forever!"

Penny, who was cradling her wrist, saw her mom hurry over to her, a worried expression on her face. "Are you all right?"

"I fell on my wrist," Penny said apologetically, holding out her hand.

Her mother inspected the swollen joint. "We'll have your father take a look at it."

A big mustached fireman in a yellow jacket walked over to where Mrs. McHale stood sobbing. "Really, ma'am," the fireman said in a husky voice. "Your house is fine. The fire never even reached the back fence. We have a team back there in the woods right now putting out the rest of it. It's under control."

"Thank heavens!" Mrs. McHale exclaimed.

Penny saw how the fireman looked them over, saw them through his eyes: a bunch of sooty, bare-chested kids who looked like they had been up to no good.

"You kids do this?" He pulled off his heavy hat and scratched his head.

"No way," Mac said.

"You think someone started it on purpose?" Penny asked.

"Sure looks that way."

"Man," Benji said, almost to himself.

"You boys ever smoke cigarettes back there?" the fireman asked.

"No," Benji said, shooting Mac a warning glance.

"Well, something started that fire. And I suspect it was of the two-legged variety," the fireman said. "We found these."

He held out a pack of blackened cigarettes.

Teddy's eyes widened at the sight.

"You recognize these, son? These yours, maybe?" the fireman asked.

"Uh, no," Teddy whispered.

The fireman gave them all a long appraising look. "Well, if you think of anything, you be sure to give us a holler. This was a real close call. If we hadn't caught the fire as quickly as we did, it could've burned down the whole block."

Mrs. McHale twisted her hands and then clutched the fireman's arm. In a desperate voice she said, "It was Caleb Devlin."

"Now, see here, Faith," Officer Cox began, in a placating tone.

Before he could get another word out, Mrs. McHale shouted, "I tell you it was Caleb! He did it before. He burned those woods years ago!"

A soft murmur went through the crowd.

The fireman looked at Officer Cox, and then Mrs. McHale, and then back at Officer Cox again.

"Calm down, Faith. You're getting yourself all worked up," Officer Cox said, holding up his hands in a soothing manner. "You know how dry it's been."

Mrs. McHale shook her head, her voice tinged with hysteria. "You know what he did to that boy! He put him in a coma! What are you waiting for? For him to burn us all out of house and home?"

"Faith—"

She whirled around, wild-eyed, and screamed, her voice echoing clear down the block, "He's going to kill someone!"

"It was a horror show," Penny's mother said to her father, describing the scene that had taken place that afternoon. "She just kept screaming, 'It was Caleb! It was Caleb!'"

They were eating dinner. Chicken, mashed potatoes, and peas. Baby Sam had smeared what looked like an entire bowl of mashed potatoes down the front of his snuggly suit.

"So, I hear you kids were in the woods," her father said in a deceptively calm voice.

Penny wanted to lie, but everyone knew that they had been in the woods. She had the sprained wrist to prove it.

"The fort——," she began.

Her father cleared his throat. "I don't want you kids to play down in the woods anymore."

"How come?" Penny asked.

"Because I said so, because I'm the dad. Can't you guys play on the street or in the yards?"

"It's not the same."

"Come on, now. Your mom doesn't like the idea of you playing back in the woods."

"So many things can happen back there. And what about the creek? I know that you're swimming in the creek, despite what I told you," her mother added, as if suddenly remembering all the times Penny and Teddy had come home with damp hair that Penny had explained away as being wet from sweat or a garden hose.

"We don't swim in the creek!" Penny said quickly.

Teddy looked morosely at his plate, digging a tunnel under his mashed potatoes and hiding the peas in it.

"Teddy, eat your peas," Mrs. Carson said.

"Look, tell you what," Penny's father cajoled her. "How about I build you guys a fort? Right here in your own backyard?"

Penny and Teddy looked at him dubiously.

"With a rope?" Teddy asked.

"Sure, why not?" Dr. Carson said easily. "And a fireman's pole, too, if that's what you want."

Teddy brightened a little.

"So, we understand each other, right, kids? You guys will stay out of the woods?" Penny's father said, like it was all settled.

They nodded, but beneath the table they tapped each other's feet. Taps that said what parents didn't know wouldn't hurt them.

They saw the full extent of the damage the next morning. A swath of woods extending up toward the McHales' had been burned, and the fort was a smoldering carcass.

"What a mess," Mac said angrily, winging a burned piece of two-by-four at a tree. He was in a grim mood. It had taken incredible stealth just to get out of his house.

"All my comic books," Benji said in a broken voice.

"Mine, too," Mac spit out.

Benji took a deep breath. "At least the BB guns weren't here."

"Or the fireworks," Oren added with relief.

Penny didn't even want to think what would have happened if there had been fireworks in the fort when that fire was going.

Zachary came crashing through the woods. He didn't have a sling on anymore, Penny noticed. Her own wrist felt much better. He stopped when he saw the burned fort, and his mouth dropped open.

"Man," he said, looking shaken. "Caleb did this?"

"No kidding, Sherlock," Mac said sarcastically.

"What are we gonna do?" Zachary asked, looking at them all.

"We?" Mac echoed.

Zachary looked flustered.

Penny whirled on Mac. "Leave him alone!"

Mac looked at the burned fort and shook his head in disgust. "Let's get out of here. This place stinks," he said bitterly.

"Yeah," Teddy said, his face pale.

Penny knew that they believed her now. She knew it without even having to ask, by the look in their eyes. And something else. They were angry, really angry.

It was war.

They set off down the creek bed, away from the burned ruins of that part of the woods. As they walked along, one side of the bank grew higher and steeper until it was far above them.

There was a crackling noise in the distance, like a deer breaking a branch, and they all leaped at the sound, hearts pounding.

"What was that?" Zachary whispered.

They all ignored him.

"I bet he knew we were at the fort and tried to get us on purpose," Penny said. "What did your mom mean, Mac, about him starting a fire in the woods years ago?"

"There was a fire, back past the skeet range, and Toby saw Caleb leaving the woods right after it started," Mac said. "It was a long time ago."

There was a soft noise, and Benji looked up.

"Oh, jeez," Benji whispered under his breath. He turned to the other kids and held a finger to his lips, waving with the other hand and then pointing up. From high above them came the voices of two boys.

"Yo, Caleb. Check it out. Must've gotten burned in the fire," a voice chortled. Penny recognized it immediately. It was that kid Doug Coles, who was always selling drugs under the Lark Hill bridge.

"Extra crispy," Caleb said in a husky drawl. Then he laughed.

Penny held her body flat to the cliff wall on the steep side of the creek, the smell of cigarette smoke drifting down to her. When she looked up, she saw the broad stretch of Caleb's back, the hard outline of his thighs, encased in filthy old jeans, the muscled arms visible beneath the black T-shirt. His dark hair was a little too long, so that it curled at the nape of his neck, and a part of her wanted to reach out and touch it, just to see what it felt like.

"Let me have it," Doug said.

Something came flying over the edge, and to her horror, Penny recognized it at once. A charred turtle shell, the soft turtle part burned away. Penny gasped audibly, watching the turtle shell fall.

"You hear something?" Doug asked.

"Nah," Caleb said. "Let's go." And then they walked away, their voices fading in the distance.

The kids huddled around the black shell. Teddy's eyes welled with tears.

"Ahh, man," Mac said glumly.

It was Tom Ten.

"It's okay, Teddy," Penny said half-heartedly, not even believing her own words.

In a dull voice Teddy repeated Caleb's cruel words—"Extra crispy"—and then started to cry.

CHAPTER 9

What else do we need?" Teddy asked as they dug around the garage for spare tools. He waved a rusty hammer, orangy-brown on the edges. "There's no way Dad's going to miss this one."

"We could really use his good screwdriver, but he would definitely miss that," Penny said, pocketing a wrench.

"How about this?" Teddy asked, holding a short, rusty saw.

"Sure." Penny hefted her backpack, weighted down now with tools. "Let's go."

They stepped out of the garage and a wave of heat hit them, thick and suffocating as an old quilt. Penny looked across the street and wondered if Amy was swimming at the public pool with her new, older friends.

Penny and Teddy walked out of the backyard and right into the woods, something they wouldn't have dared to do if their mother had been home. But she had left to go to the grocery store after breakfast, and wouldn't be back for a while.

"Have you seen Mr. Cat?" Mrs. Carson had asked curiously that morning, eyeing his food bowl.

Penny had hesitated. Surely her mother would believe her? But then she considered that she had seen Mr. Cat while she was down at the creek, somewhere she was not supposed to be—and after the fire, she knew that admitting she'd been in the creek was a bad idea.

"Uh, no," Penny had said.

The woods were cool after the bright heat of the sun. After the scare yesterday with Caleb and Doug, Penny and the boys had unanimously decided to rebuild their fort much deeper in the woods, far from Caleb's old stomping grounds. Mac, with his infinite resources, had located a new source for lumber, a building site a few blocks from Wren Circle, and the boys were already there, picking up the wood. Well, actually they were stealing it, but Penny didn't like to think about that.

They reached the location of the new fort, a high

stretch along the creek, far from the burned part of the woods. Penny dropped her backpack and started to pull out the tools.

"Darn," Penny said. "I forgot to bring nails."

"I'll go back and get them," Teddy offered.

"No, you stay here. The guys'll be here any minute and you can help them. Don't go wandering off, okay?" she said.

"I won't, *Mom*," he said.

She trotted off through the woods at a jog, wending her way back up to their house. The minivan was still missing from the driveway, so she went into the garage. There were several boxes of nails, and she stole a few nails from each of them, filling the pockets of her shorts until they bulged. Then she headed back through the dark, cool woods.

Penny was out of breath when she finally reached the clearing. And Teddy was nowhere in sight.

"Teddy?" she called, a frisson of fear running up her spine.

Silence.

"Teddy!" she shouted. "This isn't funny!"

Her only response was chirping birds. Teddy wouldn't wander away for no reason at all, would he? Maybe he was going to the bathroom—yes, that was it!

"Teddy!"

But what if something bad had happened? She should never have left him alone! She took off into the brush, running blindly through the woods, the nails falling from her pockets to the forest floor, scattering.

She circled the clearing, calling frantically, her eyes scanning the ground, the trees, the weeds.

And then she saw it. A red tennis sneaker sticking out of the brush.

But Teddy's sneaker, Penny thought shakily, was white, not red, and the edge of the sneaker poking out of the brush was definitely red. A bright sort of red. A weird splotchy red.

She took a step closer.

Blood red.

She was running through the woods, tree branches slapping her face, her heart pounding. It was just like her nightmare, except that it was worse than anything she had ever imagined.

Teddy was lying in the woods, maybe even dying. She had tried to get the trap off by sheer force, but in the end had run back to where they had dumped the tools and gotten the wrench. When the trap had finally sprung open, the sudden release of pressure had caused Teddy to buck wildly, like a corpse come to life, shrieking in pain.

And now he was back there—unconscious, hurt, and alone!—while she ran to get help.

What if Caleb was still in the woods somewhere? The very thought caused her breath to catch, her heart to thump hard against her ribs. She heard a crackling sound behind her and looked back—and slammed right into someone, knocking herself to the ground.

"Whoa!" Zachary said, stumbling back and falling, a paper bag dropping from his hand.

"Teddy . . . ," she gasped, her voice a squeak.

Zachary stood up leisurely, brushing himself off. "What's the hurry? Are the guys already at the fort?"

"Teddy!" she wailed, feeling her chest go painfully tight.

"Penny?" Zachary asked, wide-eyed.

She gasped, trying to catch her breath, desperation rising in her. *Teddy was back there in the woods and she couldn't even help him!*

Zachary scrambled around the forest floor desperately. "Here," he said, shaking the paper bag, sending newly bought sandpaper flying. He pushed the empty bag into her hands. "Here."

Penny breathed in and out of the paper bag and

felt her lungs cooperate.

Zachary hunkered down in front of her. "You okay?"

"Teddy's hurt," she said at last, still feeling light-headed.

"Where?"

"Follow me," she said, willing herself to stand up.

Teddy was lying right where Penny had left him, his foot mangled-looking.

"Holy cow!" Zachary blurted out.

Penny started to shake, just looking at her little brother. He was so still and pale, his face white as ash. He looked dead, like Mr. Cat.

"Penny!" Zachary shouted.

She stared at him numbly.

"Come on!" Zachary urged her. "Take his shoulders."

"What?" Penny asked dully.

Zachary lifted Teddy's hips gently. "His shoulders, Penny! We have to get him help!"

Something in his voice shook her, and she snapped into action.

As they carried him out of the woods, cradled between the two of them, Teddy mumbled one word from his bloodless lips, a word that almost made

Penny drop her little brother.

"Caleb," he whispered.

"I saw him, standing over me, in the woods," Teddy said, his voice shaking with remembered fear.

The kids were arrayed around the hospital bed, in a stark room in the pediatric ward. Teddy was wearing hospital pajamas, the thin bedsheets tucked around his waist. He seemed so broken, lying in the bed, swathed in wires and tubes.

Zachary and Penny had carried Teddy all the way to the Schuylers' house, right into the kitchen. Old Mrs. Schuyler had dropped the pie she was holding when she saw Penny and Zachary standing there, swaying and white-faced, Teddy suspended between them. Penny hadn't uttered a word the whole way to the hospital. She'd just sat in the backseat of Mrs. Schuyler's car, Teddy's head cradled on her lap.

"Did he say anything?" Zachary asked, a worried expression on his face.

"I heard someone say, 'Hey kid, what are you doing with my trap?'"

Zachary pressed him. "But was it Caleb?"

"I'm not sure," Teddy whispered, his face pale. "But it had to be him," he added, as if trying to convince himself. "There was a trail blaze on the tree! A lightning bolt! That's what I was looking at when I stepped in the trap."

The kids nodded grimly. They had all gone back to the spot and seen the freshly carved lightning bolt on the tree, so new the exposed wood was still green.

The antiseptic hospital smell of the room invaded Penny's nose. She went to the window and looked out at the beautiful sunny day, the sky blue and bright. It was all her fault, she thought. She should never have left Teddy alone in the woods. She had overheard her parents talking in the hospital corridor. Her mother had just wept and wept and wept. "I should've listened to you about Caleb," her mother had said in an agonized voice to her father.

"How's your foot?" Benji asked.

Teddy's foot, suspended above the bed in a sling, was wrapped in a plaster cast. Teddy winced. "It's broken. I'm gonna have the cast on for at least six weeks, Dad said, and maybe even longer. And I have to use crutches. This is gonna ruin my summer."

"That's a pain," Benji said.

"Did you tell the police you saw Caleb?" Oren asked quietly.

Teddy bit his lip, saying nothing.

"Police? Why bother?" Mac snorted. "They can't do anything."

Penny knew that Mac was right. Officer Cox and a young cherub-faced recruit fresh out of the academy had questioned Teddy the day before. She had heard the police telling her parents that there was nothing out of the ordinary, that the trap had been a run-of-the-mill animal trap that you could pick up at any hunting store. A very popular model, in fact.

"Good for foxes," the young police officer had said, as if he'd set a few himself.

"It's illegal to set traps back there out of season, but a lot of the local hunters do anyway, and there's just too much land to cover. If you have any idea who might have set it, I can look into it, but otherwise the best thing to do is just keep your kids out of the woods," Officer Cox had suggested. "Best thing really."

A nurse poked her head into the doorway. "Visiting hours end in five minutes," she said sternly.

"Okay," Mac said, with a false cheery smile. The door swung shut, and he muttered, "Witch."

Penny's head spun. The rat. The guts. Mr. Cat. The fire. And now Teddy. There was no question in her mind anymore. It was all so clear. Caleb was after her family. After her. Something in her hardened, resolved.

"He'll never stop. Nobody's ever gonna stop him. Not the police, not our parents. Who's gonna be next?" Penny demanded, her voice rising sharply.

No one said anything.

Clutching his sheet as if it would protect him, Teddy whispered in a low voice, "The nurse said they were gonna let me out the day after tomorrow."

"Yeah?" Benji said.

Teddy nodded seriously. "But I'm thinking maybe I'll stay here."

"How's Teddy?" Benji asked several days later.

Penny and Benji were biking home from the convenience store. It was early afternoon, and the sun beat down on them in hot, stifling waves. The bike ride to the convenience store had felt twice as long in this heat. They were both soaked through with sweat.

Mac was at the dentist, and Oren had to mow the lawn now that his dad had moved out of the house, and nobody knew where Zachary was, probably being tortured by his mother in one of her "Bible groups."

"He's getting pretty good with the crutches," Penny said. They had let Teddy come home from the hospital after two days of observation. "He really wants to do the bike competition, but he doesn't get that cast off for a while."

Mr. Schuyler had organized a bike-decorating competition for the Fourth, and it was just a few days away now.

"Maybe he can, like, decorate it, and you can ride it for him," Benji suggested.

"That's a good idea," she said.

What she didn't say was how weak and pale Teddy still was, or how his nightmares had gotten worse, that a night didn't go by that he didn't wake up screaming that Caleb was going to get him. Not that she was sleeping all that well herself.

They stopped their bikes on the bridge at the base of Lark Hill, contemplating the steep slope, a hard ride even in cool weather.

"Let's take a break," Benji suggested.

Penny walked to the side of the bridge and looked down at the creek. Part of her couldn't bear to look down at the rocky creek bed because it reminded her of Mr. Cat. Where was his body? she wondered. What had Caleb done with it?

The creek was dry as a bone, studded with big, smooth rocks and old trash. A rubber tire. An aluminum can. Penny leaned over and could just see one black motorcycle boot almost directly below her. She waved at Benji to come over.

"What——?" Benji started to ask, but then stopped when Penny held a finger to her lips.

They leaned over the edge to listen to the voices echoing from beneath the bridge. For a moment she didn't catch anything, and then she heard a satisfied laugh.

"Yo, Caleb, this is good stuff," Doug Coles said, his voice sounding a little funny, sort of squeaky, like Mickey Mouse.

A pause, and then a gravelly-sounding voice said, "Best there is, right now."

"Man, I'll have no problem moving this stuff," Doug said, inhaling deeply.

The sweet smell of pot wafted up.

"Don't smoke it all," Caleb said, an edge to his voice.

"How much you got?"

"Enough."

"Cool. Everyone should be in a partying mood, the Fourth and all. Same plan?" Doug asked.

Caleb grunted in agreement. "I'm outta here."

The sound of Caleb climbing the incline toward the top of the bridge shook them, and Penny and Benji ran to their bikes and pedaled away hard, up the hill, never looking back.

They never saw Caleb Devlin turn to stare at their departing figures.

"So what?" Mac said, slamming the hockey puck across the table to Zachary, who missed. "So he's dealing drugs? Big surprise. He's moving up."

They were playing air hockey in Mac's basement, where his mother had banished them all so that she could get ready for her date in peace. The washing machine was also in the basement, so the whole room smelled of dirty socks and washing detergent and mildew.

"Who cares," Oren seconded, with such a Mac-like gesture that Penny blinked in surprise.

Mac slammed the puck into the goal. "Six-nothing!" he crowed to Zachary. "You suck."

Zachary flushed darkly.

Benji shared a frustrated look with Penny. They had rushed over to tell the boys their news, and this was not the reaction they had expected. "We just thought you guys would want to know, is all."

The humming sound of the table rose in the room.

"But the thing is, he's kind of on parole now. From

the juvie home," Zachary said carefully.

"Because of his mom?" Penny asked.

"Yeah," Zachary said. "And if he got caught with drugs on him . . . ," he added suggestively.

Mac's eyebrows went up. He turned and looked at Zachary. "They'd send him back," he said in dawning comprehension.

Zachary grinned.

Zachary still had his lame moments, but he was a lot cooler than he used to be—rescuing Teddy in the woods, and now this. The boys must be rubbing off on him, Penny decided.

"So what's the plan?" Penny asked excitedly.

Everyone turned to Mac.

Mac thought for a moment. "We have to somehow tell the cops. And get them to show up while he has the drugs in the house. That way they can bust him."

"Who's gonna call the cops?" Penny asked, worried.

"Count me out," Mac said.

"Yeah, they'll definitely recognize your voice," Benji said snidely.

Mac narrowed his eyes.

"I'll do it," Zachary said eagerly.

"You will?" Penny asked.

"I'll call from the pay phone and muffle my voice. Like they do on TV."

"Like an anonymous call?" Penny said.

"Sure," Zachary said.

"It just might work," Mac said approvingly.

The next evening a police cruiser drove down the block, interrupting the kids' softball game in the cul-de-sac. The cruiser parked in front of the Devlins' house, causing the watching parents to raise their eyebrows.

"Looks like trouble," Mr. Schuyler said, with a low whistle.

Penny nodded silently, her eyes fixed on Officer Cox.

Officer Cox stepped out of the cruiser and hiked up his pants, looking around as if suddenly noticing how everyone was watching him.

Mrs. Bukvic, who had been gossiping with the other mothers, stood up and walked over to Officer Cox, her features set in a determined expression.

Penny couldn't hear what Mrs. Bukvic was saying to Officer Cox, but she did catch "Buster" several times. Mrs. Bukvic's voice went up a pitch whenever she said her missing pet's name.

Finally Officer Cox shrugged off the angry Mrs. Bukvic, walked up to the Devlins' front door, and knocked. Mr. Devlin answered on the second knock. The front door was out of earshot, but they could see Officer Cox speaking to Mr. Devlin, and after a moment Mr. Devlin nodded and stepped aside to let Officer Cox into the house.

Nearly an hour later, the game over, the kids went into a huddle at the curb, where Mr. Schuyler was sitting, drinking a beer. Most of the parents had drifted away.

"He's been in there a long time," Penny said in a worried voice.

Mac banged a metal bat against the curb. "I'm sure he hid it pretty well."

Penny stared hard at the house. "I wonder which room is his?" *What did it look like?* she thought. *Did he bring girls up there?*

"It's gonna work," Benji said. "I can feel it."

"Anyone want a piece of gum?" Zachary asked, all nervous excitement.

The screen door suddenly opened, and Officer Cox stepped out onto the porch.

"Hey," Mac said. "Where's Caleb? Why isn't he hauling out Caleb?"

"There he is!" Penny said urgently.

Caleb stepped out with his father. Mr. Devlin gave Officer Cox a short handshake, and then put his arm around Caleb's shoulders.

"Sorry about that," Officer Cox said loudly, walking toward his patrol car.

Mr. Devlin just nodded. "No problem."

"You folks have a good evening, okay?" Officer Cox said.

"We'll try," Caleb said, shooting a hard, knowing look at the kids huddled at the curb. His eyes flicked over the group, settling on Penny's shocked face.

And then he winked.

CHAPTER 10

I'm telling you, he looked right at me. He *knows* we were the ones who called the cops!" Penny said, pacing back and forth.

It was the next morning, and Penny and the boys were in Teddy's bedroom, rehashing their abysmal failure of the previous evening. Teddy, reclining on his bed like a pasha, his foot propped up on a pillow, was looking a little pale as they recounted the events.

"He doesn't know," Mac scoffed.

"What are you guys doing?" Penny's mom called through the door in a suspicious voice. "It's too quiet in there."

"Nothing," Penny said. "It's secret. No moms allowed."

"This mom is always allowed. Open up."

Penny reluctantly opened the door.

Her mother stood there, a no-nonsense look on her face. "Listen, I'm taking the baby and running over to the dry cleaner's and then meeting Mrs. Loew for lunch. If you need anything, go over to the Schuylers' house. And under no circumstances are *any* of you kids to go into those woods, you got me? Caleb is a dangerous boy." She looked hard at Penny in particular. "Got it?"

"Keep the doors locked, and Penny, use your own key. Leave the spare one under the rock where it's supposed to be," her mother added.

"Sure," Penny said.

The door closed, and the kids looked at one another.

"You don't have to tell me twice," Oren said.

Penny heard the minivan back out and drive away. A few moments later, she heard screeching tires. Had her mom come back? She got up and walked over to the window, peering through the curtains her mother had sewn herself when they first moved in. Teddy's room faced onto the street, with a clear view of the Bukvics' driveway.

The very same driveway where a red Trans Am was now parked.

Penny watched as the driver's door of the Trans

Am opened and a bare arm holding a cigarette tapped ash on the driveway. Caleb unfolded his long lean figure and got out of the car. Then he slammed the car door shut and walked up to the Bukvics' front door, opening it casually and walking right in, as if he'd done it a hundred times.

Penny blinked. She couldn't believe what she'd just seen! Maybe it was a mirage or a hallucination or something.

Except the Trans Am was still parked right there in the driveway.

And then the front door opened and Caleb stepped out, Amy Bukvic draped on his arm.

"You guys," Penny said in a shaky voice.

Teddy looked up, alarmed by the tone of his sister's voice. "What?"

"Just come here," she said to the others.

She pointed out the window. The boys gathered around, looking out.

Amy Bukvic, wearing a skimpy tank top and tight jeans, had slid her hand into Caleb's back pocket in a proprietary way. Her hair was plastered with about a pound of hairspray, so that when it hit the humidity, it barely drooped.

Benji yelped, "Caleb and Amy?"

Amy's tank top bounced suggestively with each step she took.

"Unbelievable," Oren said, shaking his head, his mouth open in disbelief.

Mac stared at Amy's chest through slit eyes.

Caleb shut the door of Amy's house and surveyed the quiet block. Penny held her breath as he stared at the Carsons', his piercing dark eyes searching it, and for a brief moment Penny thought maybe he'd seen them.

"Get down," she whispered, panicked.

They flattened themselves on the carpet. A few seconds later they heard the Trans Am roar up the street.

"No way he could see us," Zachary whispered.

"Why are you whispering?" Mac said.

"Whose car is it?" Benji asked. "It's never parked in the Devlins' driveway."

"I know whose it is," Mac said. "That kid who's always dealing under the bridge. Doug Coles."

Penny didn't say anything. She just sat there, reeling from the revelation, trying to imagine what it was like to be Amy.

The one who kissed the devil.

The kids were ready with their bikes the next morning when the red Trans Am appeared outside the Bukvics' house. Amy got in, and the Trans Am roared out of the driveway in a flurry of screeching tires. The kids set off after it on their bikes, pedaling furiously to keep up with the car. They followed from a safe distance, but it was hard work, and when the car screeched to a stop at the small shopping area less than a mile away, they were relieved. They stood there for a moment, trying to catch their breath, gasping in the late-morning sun, the blacktop hot beneath their feet and the scent of tar starting to stick in their noses.

Caleb stepped out of the car, all long hard legs. They saw Amy beckon him toward her open window, reach up to wind her arms around his neck, and say in a high false voice, "Don't keep me waiting long."

The kids recoiled.

"I'm gonna barf," Oren said, clutching his stomach. " 'Don't keep me waiting,' " he mimicked.

"Where's he going?" Penny asked.

"Probably the liquor store," Mac predicted.

Benji darted off behind Caleb. "I'm gonna see."

They watched as Caleb strode with long lanky steps, not to the liquor store, but to the hardware store. Benji slipped into the store behind him.

Penny turned to Mac. "The hardware store?"

"Maybe he's buying a gun," Oren suggested.

"You can't buy a gun at a hardware store," Mac said in a disparaging tone.

"You can buy shells," Oren said.

Mac scoffed. "You can buy shot, not shells," he said, ever the expert.

Penny, who thought they were both talking out their ears, said, "I'll be right back."

"Penny, don't!" Zachary cautioned her, but she was already gone, moving fast toward the red Trans Am, sneaking up behind it.

Amy was sitting in the front seat, the passenger-side vanity mirror flipped down, elaborately applying brown mascara. Penny watched, fascinated. Where had she learned how to do this? Amy expertly applied a thick coat to her top eyelashes, and then looked up, dabbing the mascara on the lower eyelashes.

"Penny!" Zachary called in a loud whisper, and Penny whirled around to see the boys gesturing furiously at her. She took a last glance at Amy and then took off toward the boys. Benji was standing in their midst, talking excitedly about Caleb.

"He bought a shovel, and some rope, and a huge ax. Look!" Benji pointed.

Sure enough, Caleb was walking out of the hardware store with a coil of rope looped around his shoulder, a long shovel swung over it, and an ax with a shiny new blade in his other hand.

"What's the ax for?" Penny asked.

"To chop us up," Oren said.

"And the shovel?"

"To bury our dead bodies!" Zachary said.

Not to mention Mr. Cat and Buster and all those other pets, Penny thought darkly.

They watched as Caleb popped open the trunk and tossed the stuff in. Then he returned to the driver's seat, revved up the motor, and spun the car out of the parking lot, leaving the kids in its dust.

"I wish we could just kill him first," Mac said in a low fierce voice.

"Yeah," Oren echoed.

They looked at one another, realization dawning on their faces, possibility in the air.

"Whoa," Zachary exclaimed, holding his hands up as if to slow them all down. "You can't just walk up and kill him. Look what happened to me! And, and— Teddy!"

"Yeah, not to mention that Jeffy kid," Penny pointed out.

"Accidents happen all the time," Oren said quietly, thoughtfully, the ghost of a smile on his face.

Mac snapped his fingers. "The Trans Am."

"What about the Trans Am?" Benji asked.

"We cut the brakes on the Trans Am," Mac said, like it was so simple, like it was something he did every day. "That'd be justice, same way he killed his own sister."

"I don't know," Benji said.

Mac ignored him, his face starting to flush with excitement. "We cut the brakes when he's parked across the street visiting Amy, and then he, well . . ."

"Crashes," Oren finished in a cool voice.

"Yeah," Mac said. "It's cake." He looked at each of them. "Well?"

Penny nodded. It wasn't a bad plan. And best of all, it didn't require any direct contact with Caleb. "Okay. But who's gonna do it?"

"You guys are serious?" Zachary asked.

"Two people should go," Mac said. "The other three will be lookouts."

"Let's do Rock, Paper, Scissors," Benji said. "It's the only fair way."

Mac and Benji put their fists up.

"On three," Oren said. "One, two, three!"

Mac's hand was a rock, Benji's a pair of scissors. Mac tapped Benji's hand with his fist. "Rock smashes scissors."

Benji gulped and then smiled bravely. "Looks like I'm in."

"You and Penny next," Mac said, staring at Zachary.

"But . . . ," Zachary began.

"You gonna wimp out?" Mac asked in a low voice. "Penny's not scared."

Zachary bit his lip worriedly and put his fist up. So did Penny.

"One, two, three!"

Zachary smiled, relief shining on his face. "Rock—"

"Smashes scissors," Penny finished grimly. She hated Rock, Paper, Scissors. She always lost. "Okay, Oren, let's do it."

Oren had a hard look on his face, his fist clenched as if he was looking forward to a good fight and Caleb was just the guy.

"One, two, three!"

Penny and Oren flung their hands out in front of them.

Oren looked up at Penny, a frustrated expression

on his face. "Scissors cut paper."

Penny looked down at her fingers, splayed flat like paper.

"Yeah," she said, "I know."

The next morning, the kids waited in the Carsons' garage in nervous anticipation. Penny had rifled through her dad's tools, looking for shears or clippers or anything thick enough to cut through hose. Her mother had taken the baby and gone to the grocery store.

Penny felt awful. She'd been so worried and full of dread that she'd barely eaten her dinner the night before and hadn't touched her breakfast—she knew that if she put anything in her stomach, it was just going to come right back up. Penny looked longingly at her new bike sitting in the corner of the garage. The Fourth of July was tomorrow, and she still had to decorate the bike for the competition.

Teddy's bike, done up in an astronaut theme, was almost finished, thanks to their dad, who had seemingly poured all his guilt and anxiety over Teddy's accident into helping Teddy with the decorations. In fact, the accident had made Penny's parents pretty hysterical lately. The kids were forbidden to go anywhere without telling them. No more just stepping out of the house and playing.

"Do you think Caleb killed Buster? Like Mrs. Bukvic keeps saying?" Penny had asked her mother the previous night.

"Maybe," her mother had said, her eyes worried.

Penny almost told her mother then and there about Mr. Cat, but some instinct had made her hold her tongue. What could she tell her, after all? What proof did she have? Mr. Cat took off all the time. Her mother would just chalk it up to anxiety, and not let her play outside at all.

"What's taking him so long?" Mac asked in a frustrated voice. Penny thought that Mac wouldn't be in such a hurry if he was the one who had to go across the street.

"Maybe he won't come today," Penny said, half to herself.

"He'll come," Mac said.

She heard screeching tires, and Oren hissed, "He's here! Get ready, you guys."

The Trans Am was sitting in the Bukvics' driveway, like a red tomato ripening in the sun. Caleb climbed out and sauntered through the front door.

"Time to go," Benji said. "Got the tools?"

Penny nodded shakily, clutching the heavy clippers.

"You okay?" Benji asked, taking in her white face.

"Yeah."

"Don't worry," Zachary assured Penny and Benji. "I'll whistle if I see him come back out."

"Okay, let's do it."

They took off across the street, dropping low when they reached the Bukvics' driveway and scuttling up to the Trans Am like crabs. They lay on their backs and inched their way across the hot blacktop under the car, Penny's heart beating a million miles a minute. Heat radiated off the engine in gasoline-tinged waves, and Benji was sweating like a fiend.

"Now what do we do?" Penny asked, breathing hard.

"Hand me the clippers," he ordered, like a surgeon at an operating table.

She slapped them into his outstretched hand. Benji stared up at the mess of tubes and wires above him.

"Hurry!" she said, fear making her voice shake.

Benji held the clippers to a piece of black tubing and then paused. He turned to Penny, his face strained. "I don't know which one to cut."

"What do you mean? I thought you asked your dad."

He shook his head in frustration. "I did, but I don't see anything like what he was talking about."

Penny took a deep breath and said, "Cut them all!"

"But—"

"Just do it!" she whispered fiercely.

He nodded shortly and cut through a thick black tube.

Blue windshield-washer fluid rained down on them. It got into Penny's mouth and soaked her shirt. She spit it out.

"Jeez!" Benji cursed, wiping his eyes.

Penny looked past Benji, feeling faint.

A pair of boots was standing there.

Benji caught the look in Penny's eyes and froze.

She pinched her eyes shut for a moment, hoping the boots would be gone when she opened them.

They weren't.

Then she heard Zachary's whistle, but it was too late—the windshield-washer fluid was already rushing out from under the car, pooling on the blacktop, flowing around Caleb's heavy black motorcycle boots. Penny watched in horrified fascination as the fluid ran down the driveway in a weirdly blue stream, shimmering iridescently.

Caleb said, "What the—?"

"Go!" Benji mouthed in a low urgent voice, shoving Penny in the direction away from Caleb. She rolled onto her belly, the windshield-washer fluid soaking her straight through, and crawled out from under the car, Benji right behind her.

Benji was just about out from under the car when Caleb's hand grabbed his foot.

"What are you doing to my car?" Caleb glowered at Benji, but Benji just kicked hard, hitting Caleb in the face. Caleb roared in shock, and then Benji was off and he and Penny were running up the street, as fast as their legs could carry them.

"Hey!" Caleb shouted.

They rounded the curve on Lark Hill Road and were gone.

CHAPTER 11

Penny and the boys were somewhat calmer by the time they scrambled into Mr. Schuyler's pristine yellow pickup truck that evening, just as the sun was setting.

Mr. Schuyler kept the truck in perfect condition for just such occasions. Usually a trip to Wallaby Farms required some sort of chore in return, and as tomorrow was the Fourth of July block party, he had a list ready for them. In return for free ice cream, the kids were going to have to help out.

"Now, you critters hold on tight," he warned. "I don't want any personal injury lawyers sniffing after me!"

Mr. Schuyler, outfitted in worn blue overalls and a John Deere cap, drove his truck at a sedate pace. But when he reached the Farm Road, on the outskirts of the neighborhood, Mr. Schuyler hit the gas and the truck went flying down the dirt road, hitting every bump and pothole, causing the kids in the back to bounce around, taking their breath away.

"This is better than the roller coaster!" Zachary shouted exuberantly, clinging to the side.

In spite of all the excitement, Penny was silent. But then, she had a lot on her mind.

After Penny's near-death experience with Caleb that morning, her mother had returned home, corralled her into the minivan with Baby Sam, and driven them to the mall. Her mother was on a mission to get Penny a dress for the Fourth of July block party. She had dragged Penny to the girls' section of a large department store and sat outside the curtained dressing room, bouncing Sam on her knee, while Penny tried on a daisy-patterned cotton sundress.

"This is a stupid dress," Penny had said sulkily from behind the curtain. She couldn't believe her mom was making her do this.

"Come out and let me see it on you."

Penny had walked out reluctantly, slouching her shoulders, her arms crossed defensively in front of her flat chest.

"You look lovely, honey," her mom had said encouragingly. "It's the perfect sort of dress for a summer party."

"I look stupid."

Her mother had looked at her and murmured, in a soft voice, "I'll bet Amy will be wearing a dress."

Penny had stared at herself in the mirror. The simple sundress made her look even younger than she was. She imagined what Amy would wear. Nothing like this, she knew instinctively. Why was she even trying?

"The boys are gonna make fun of me."

"No, they won't. Come on, it would make your dad so happy if his little girl wore a dress one day of her life." Her mother had stood behind her and smoothed her hair back, squeezing her shoulder. "You look so pretty. Don't you feel pretty in this dress?"

Penny had looked at her mother, standing behind her in the mirror, and known that she could never hope to be as beautiful as her mother, whose heavy fall of hair was shiny as a buttercup. Penny knew that even with this dress, even with a million dresses, she would never come close. She would never be the one boys stopped to admire.

And then there was no more time to think about the shopping trip, because they were at Wallaby Farms. The kids fell over one another to get in line at the old-fashioned marble counter, where stout-looking women spooned out obscenely huge scoops of ice cream. After they'd all gotten their cones, Mr. Schuyler piled them back into the truck and drove them to a big empty field not far down the road. They took their cones and sat on the grass, watching the stars start to come out.

Mr. Schuyler looked around appraisingly. "This was my farm. This piece of land was my family's farm for over one hundred years," he said.

"We know," the kids chimed in.

"And do you know who owns it now?" he asked.

"The government!" Penny shouted, in unison with everyone else. Mr. Schuyler gave the same speech every time.

"You got it, boys! The United States Federal Government," he said, emphasizing the word "federal." "Just you remember that. Don't ever trust no one, not even the government. The only person you can count on being true to you is yourself. You hear me?"

"Yes, Mr. Schuyler."

A cicada chirped mournfully.

"Can you trust policemen?" asked Penny, remembering Officer Cox.

"Nope."

"But if you can't trust policemen, who can you trust?" Teddy asked, a smear of strawberry ice cream on his thin cheek.

"Yeah," Benji said. "And what about firemen?"

"What about the FBI?" Mac said.

"And the Secret Service?" Oren added.

Mr. Schuyler sighed heavily. "Nope, you can't trust any of them. Nothing but thieves and liars, every one. They'll steal your farm, sell your tractors, slaughter your livestock."

"But what if something bad happens?" Penny whispered tremulously, the shadow of Caleb looming large over them all, a specter in the dark, a harsh whisper on the wind. "Who do we tell if something really bad happens?"

A frog croaked nearby. Zachary seemed to curl into himself, his chocolate cone forgotten.

"Well, I guess you can always tell me, but I'm not gonna be here forever." Mr. Schuyler scratched his scraggly gray beard. "Nope. One day you'll learn: the only person you can really count on is yourself."

On the way home, Mr. Schuyler managed to hit every single pothole on the Farm Road. Penny was having a hard time keeping her ice cream down.

"Your dad coming to the block party tomorrow?" Penny asked Oren.

Oren stared ahead into the darkness, his dark hair

framing his face rakishly, so that he looked like a pirate. "I don't know. My mom told him to stay away," he said.

"Do you see him much?" she asked, clinging to the side of the truck, forcing herself to keep talking to take her mind off her nausea. If Mr. Schuyler kept driving like this, she was going to barf all over the bed of the truck.

"He's always busy with his stupid girlfriend. I can't believe he won't come home with all the stuff that's going on with Caleb! I thought he'd come home! How can he leave us by ourselves? How can he?" he asked, his voice breaking.

The truck hit a massive pothole, and all the kids were thrown into the air.

"Ugh," Penny said, as she felt the ice cream slosh around in her stomach.

"I hate her!" Oren said vehemently, his black curls flopping on his forehead.

Penny met his eyes, and almost flinched at the emotion simmering there. "Who?"

"My dad's girlfriend." He looked at her and said, "I hate her guts."

And then it appeared.

The sleek red car roared out of the pitch dark,

engine roaring throatily, a demon from hell with its headlights glowing eerily like disembodied eyes. Clouds of fumes billowed behind it, and music was blasting from the stereo. A lazy arm hung out the driver's side window holding a bottle of beer, and the kids didn't need to see the skull tattoo on the back of the hand to know who it was.

"Teddy!" Penny shouted, scrambling to the rear window of the cab, where Teddy was sitting with Mr. Schuyler. She banged furiously for Teddy's attention.

The driver of the car gunned its engine and nosed up to touch the back bumper of the truck.

"He's going to hit us!" Oren yelled.

There was grinding as the two vehicles met.

"What's going on back there?" Mr. Schuyler hollered.

"Drive faster! Drive faster!" Penny shouted to Teddy through the cab window.

"What?" Teddy asked.

"It's Caleb!"

Teddy craned around, looking out the window. The arm hanging out the car behind them lifted the beer in a silent toast.

He paled and then hauled himself over to Mr. Schuyler's side and yelled in his ear, "Hurry, Mr.

Schuyler! The car behind us is bad news!"

"You got it, boy," the old man said. "Hit my truck, will ya?"

Mr. Schuyler hit the gas and accelerated for the curve ahead, spurred on by the kids in the back shouting for him to hurry. The Trans Am was nearly on top of them now. Penny clung to the side of the truck, and all she could do was stare at that muscled arm. The car kept trying to pass them, weaving dangerously back and forth, nearly forcing the truck into a gully.

"Wanna play, do you?" Mr. Schuyler shouted. "No punk kid is going to get the best of Al Schuyler! I'll show you what's what!"

"All right!" Mac shouted with a grin. "This is more like it!"

"Hold on!" Mr. Schuyler cried, eyeing the approaching curve.

Penny braced herself.

Mr. Schuyler took the curve, braking slightly, then turned the wheel hard so that the truck went sailing off the main road and onto an old dirt cattle path. The truck skidded to a stop in a cloud of dust as the car sped by, a beer bottle sailing out of it to land with a crash on the road.

"Hooligan!" Mr. Schuyler shouted, waving a fist

out the window of the cab.

Teddy was still gripping the dashboard, his knuckles white.

"You okay, boy?"

Teddy nodded, gritting his teeth.

Mr. Schuyler leaned through the cab's rear window to survey the kids in the back of the truck. He looked at their pale faces.

"You kids okay back there?" Mr. Schuyler shouted.

"Yeah, we're okay," Penny said with a gulp. "Just great."

And watched as Zachary barfed up his chocolate ice cream, along with chunks of cone and rainbow sprinkles.

CHAPTER 12

The Fourth of July dawned hot and humid, the air as sticky and moist as the gym showers at school after ball practice.

Penny was in the garage, helping Teddy put the finishing touches on his astronaut-themed bike. She had gotten up at the crack of dawn and decorated her own bike, twining black and yellow crepe paper around the spokes of the wheels, constructing long antennae out of aluminum foil, and fashioning a stinger from a sharp sliver of wood that she had painted black. It was long and thick and tapered down to a sharp point.

Her mother had seemed a little unsure about the wood. "Isn't that stinger thing a little sharp?"

"Exactly," Penny had said. "It's a bee."

Her parents had exchanged a worried look.

Now she was nearly done with Teddy's bike.

"No, put it there," Teddy ordered from his perch on the stool.

She glue-gunned silver tinsel to the spoke of a wheel.

"Okay?" she asked.

"Yeah. I can't wait to set off the fireworks," he said.

The kids were going to take the fireworks they had been stashing in the hollow tree along with them to the municipal park later that day, where the town was staging its own fireworks display. Mac figured a few more fireworks wouldn't be noticed in the noise and confusion, and they could always disappear into the crowd if anyone gave them trouble.

Teddy, Penny knew, was excited to be out and about, even if he was on crutches. He had been keeping a low profile since his accident, but nothing was going to ruin the Fourth for him. Or her, she thought, feeling light for the first time in days, excitement rushing through her veins. She would not think of Caleb today, she promised herself.

"Now go ride around the driveway," Teddy ordered. "I want to see how it looks."

Penny hopped onto the bike, pedaled out of the garage, and whirled around the driveway. The aluminum foil glinted in the bright sun.

Teddy grinned happily.

It was going to be a great day.

Maybe it was the presence of so many adults, the implied safety of the crowd, but whatever it was, Penny didn't give Caleb a second thought. It was as if she were having a day of amnesia. She had better things to think about, like sparklers and birch beer and water-balloon fights. It was, after all, a holiday.

There was tons of food: steamer clams, foot-long hot dogs, Polish kielbasa, hamburgers, macaroni salad, potato salad, deviled eggs, potato chips, and a whole cooler devoted to Popsicles for the kids. There was a keg of beer for the hardworking fathers and mothers and a keg of birch beer for the thirsty kids. Ice was scarce, and the parents collectively agreed that they needed a cold one more than the kids did, so the kids had to make do with warm birch beer.

The day moved along at a fast clip. To his delight, Teddy's astronaut bike won the contest. The potato-sack race proved amusing when Mrs. Bukvic fell flat on her ample rear. The water-balloon toss ended with half the block's mothers being soaked by their husbands. After that a no-holds-barred volleyball game all but ripped every blade of grass from the Schuylers' newly sodded side yard.

To no one's surprise, Zachary was stung by a bee and promptly dragged home by his mother. Oren did his best to avoid his father, who had showed up after all and brought his new girlfriend, a receptionist from the clinic who looked about eighteen. And Mr. Albright drank too much beer and fell asleep in a lawn chair on his own driveway.

Amy Bukvic made a brief appearance, and as Penny's mother had predicted, she was wearing a dress—a strapless hot-pink number that made more than one of the fathers in attendance stop and stare.

Penny, who was getting birch beer when Amy showed up, watched from the sidelines as Amy sauntered through the crowd with a distracted look on her face, as if she couldn't wait to get out of there. She caught sight of Penny at the kegs, walked over, and casually pumped herself a cup of real beer.

"So, isn't this party great?" Penny said awkwardly, looking around to see if Amy was going to get in trouble.

"New dress?" Amy said, shooting a critical look at Penny's sundress.

"Um," Penny stammered self-consciously.

"You have to stop letting your mom pick out your

clothes," Amy sniffed, obviously unimpressed.

"Uh, okay," Penny managed to reply, her cheeks burning.

"This party's pathetic. I am so out of here," Amy said.

"Where are you going?"

"To a real party, that's where. Somewhere where there aren't any parents."

"What kind of party? I mean, whose?"

"No one *you* know," Amy said, with a withering look.

Penny said in a tentative voice, "Could I—"

"No, you are *not* invited," Amy said, with a nasty grin. "No little girls allowed."

Penny blanched.

Amy tipped her head back, draining her cup. Then she dropped it on the ground and walked away. "Have a great time playing with all the *kiddies*," she called over her shoulder sarcastically.

Amy Bukvic aside, it was still the best block party ever. They all ate too much, and got sunburned, and played so hard they panted like dogs. Mrs. Bukvic, the organizer, was queen for the day, and even Officer Cox stopped by for a laugh and a hot dog. "Just keep the peace," he joked.

But the Devlins' front door, just off the cul-de-sac, stayed shut, the blinds drawn, no hint of life in the house.

Then several things happened very quickly.

The steamer clams Benji's dad had bought from a buddy in South Philly turned out to be bad. In short order Mrs. McHale, Dr. Loew, Oren, Becky, and Dr. Loew's new girlfriend were struck down with food poisoning and had to be rushed to the emergency room. Oren, Penny noticed, wore a secretly pleased expression when he observed his father's new girlfriend puking her guts up on the lawn, even though he was doing the very same thing a moment later.

Then Penny's dad's beeper went off. Two kids who lived in the trailer park out on the Farm Road had been playing with fireworks and almost succeeded in melting the skin off their arms.

Soon after her dad left, Mac, lit from the beer he'd been sneaking from the keg all day, stood in the middle of the cul-de-sac and whistled, waving at the swooping bats with a big butterfly net. He managed to catch one as it flew low, confused by his whistle; but when he reached to take it out of the net, the bat bit him hard on the cheek and then flew off into the trees.

Penny's mom was prevailed upon to render first aid—everyone assumed that she knew what to do because she was a pediatrician's wife. She knew enough to know that Mac would have go to the hospital, so she parked the baby with Mrs. Loew and drove Mac to the emergency room, where his mom was still throwing up her guts.

Benji, Teddy, and Penny watched with dismay as Mac was bundled into the Carsons' minivan.

"I told him not to mess with that bat," Teddy said, leaning on his crutches.

First Oren and now Mac. Things came in threes, Penny knew. Who would be hurt next? she wondered, and then reconsidered. Zachary had gotten stung by the bee. He sort of counted. That would make three, wouldn't it?

"Wait," Benji said, suddenly remembering something. "The fireworks are still at the creek."

It was supposed to be Mac's job to retrieve the fireworks before they went to the park, but that wasn't going to happen now.

"The sun's gonna go down soon," Penny said. "We better get them now while we can still see back there."

"Yeah," Benji agreed.

They were walking away when Mr. Schuyler called out. "Hey, you kids, come here," he hollered across the cul-de-sac. They turned around, startled. Did he mean them?

He jabbed a finger at them. "Yes, you." He was holding a box of heavy black trash bags. "Come on and help clean up this mess."

"But, Mr. Schuyler," Benji whined.

Mr. Schuyler shook his head decisively. "Don't 'Mr. Schuyler' me. This here's a block party, and you live on the block, so you gotta help clean up."

"I gotta—" Benji was tongue-tied. "It's really important," Benji finally blurted.

Mr. Schuyler snorted. "I'm sure it is," he said, thrusting the box of trash bags at him. "Make yourself useful."

Penny waited until Mr. Schuyler was out of earshot and then said, "Look, you guys start cleaning up, and I'll run down to the woods, get the fireworks, and meet you back here and help."

"You don't have enough time," Teddy said, visibly panicking. "We're supposed to go soon."

"And I'm not getting stuck doing this all by myself," Benji said irritably, giving Teddy and his crutches a disparaging toss of his head.

"Hey, I can hold the bags!" Teddy said.

"I'll be really fast," Penny promised. "Mac will kill us if we forget the fireworks. We've been planning this all summer! Just tell Mr. Schuyler I went to the bathroom."

"C'mon, kids. Get a move on it," Mr. Schuyler yelled from across the cul-de-sac. "We're leaving in half an hour."

Benji sighed. "Hurry."

"Don't let them leave without me," Penny yelled, already off at a run.

Penny trotted quickly through the woods, the sounds of the block party fading in the distance, her dress swaying gently against her legs.

The woods were full of dark pockets, where the lacy canopy of leaves and branches grew thickest. Here and there among the trees the evening's first fireflies were starting to wink on and off. By the time she returned it would be dark, and that meant it would be time to go to the municipal park. One thing was certain: she was changing out of this stupid dress.

She followed the creek along its winding path until she reached the old hollow tree by the steep cliff. She reached inside for the metal box and sighed with relief. The fireworks were right where Mac had left them, neatly packed in the plastic bag, nestled next to the BB guns. She grabbed up the bag, then closed the metal box and stowed it back in the tree.

"Whatcha got there?"

Penny went still at the sound of the voice, closing her eyes.

"Huh, kid?"

She turned around slowly, her hands shaking so hard that she dropped the bag on the ground, fireworks spilling out like candy.

Caleb Devlin stood on the edge of the cliff, the last rays of sunshine fighting their way through the thinning trees to wash over him like a golden brush. He was wearing worn jeans and an old T-shirt, a black one that hung on him, a little too big, like he'd gotten it from someone else, and it had been washed so many times it looked thin in places. The only new-looking thing he had on were black motorcycle boots, and they looked shiny, as if he took special care of them. Penny imagined him polishing those boots every night, to keep them gleaming, like new.

He nudged the fireworks with the shiny tip of a boot. "Fireworks, huh? Planning to celebrate something?"

Penny jerked her head up, taking a step back. "The Fourth," she choked out.

"Of course, the Fourth," he said, as if suddenly understanding. He pulled out the silver cigarette case and shook a cigarette out, then flicked on the lighter and drew on the cigarette. The light from the flame illuminated his face, the stubble on his cheek, the thin white scar by his eye.

He squinted at her and casually held out the pack.

"I don't smoke," Penny said, her voice sounding strained to her own ears.

"I'm not surprised." Caleb said, inhaling deeply, leaning against a tree as if he had all the time in the world. "What's your name, kid?"

"Penny Carson," she whispered.

He nodded like he knew.

"You're that girl that's always playing with the boys, aren't you?"

She nodded her head uneasily.

"So how come you're wearing a dress?" His eyes ran up and down her slender form in frank appraisal. Here was a boy used to real girls—girls with actual breasts and hips, girls like Amy.

She sucked in her breath. "Because my mom made me."

"Trying to turn you into a little lady?" he asked with a not-very-nice sort of laugh.

"I guess." Penny's mind was whirling. She was all alone in the woods, too far back for anyone to hear her scream, even.

"You guess, huh?"

Penny took a step forward, trying to sidestep around him.

He grinned at her, shaking his head as if she had somehow disappointed him. "Where do you think you're going?"

"I have to get back. Everyone's waiting for me," she said in a shaky voice.

He grabbed her by the elbow and dragged her roughly back to where he stood.

"Is that so?" he said, his voice like gravel. He pulled deeply on the cigarette and stared at her hard, his eyelashes so lush they should have been on a girl.

She nodded, fear bright on her face.

"Well, they're just gonna have to wait." Caleb flicked the cigarette onto the dirt, grinding it with his boot. "See, I have a few questions I want to ask you, Penny Carson."

Penny paled.

"Like what do you do with those boys all the

time?" he asked in a deceptively casual voice.

"Play," she whispered.

"Play? Games? Like spin the bottle?" he laughed.

"No."

"You like boys, Penny?"

He came and stood next to her, so close she felt the heat coming off his body. He ran his hand lightly up her arm so that the fine hairs stood up, a rush of sensation tingling up her spine. She couldn't move.

"Huh?" he said, right into her ear, his breath hot and moist, like steam. He nipped lightly at her earlobe. "You like boys?" he asked in a husky voice.

"I don't know," she gasped, overwhelmed by the feel of him, so close. He smelled of tobacco and something musky, like sweat.

Caleb laughed throatily. "Don't know, huh?"

Penny stared into his eyes. They were a soft gray-green color with gold flecks. *So beautiful,* she almost said aloud. He smiled at her, revealing a chipped tooth, but even that tooth seemed right, somehow, on him.

Caleb's hand smoothed the soft skin of her neck, rubbing it as if he was a sculptor and she was a statue just waiting for him to breathe life into her. He nuzzled the edge of her collarbone, teeth scraping.

"I like this dress," he whispered.

His hand was heavy on her shoulder, and she could feel him playing with the zipper at the back of her dress, tugging it up and down an inch, and that tinny little sound shook her like nothing else could. She started to struggle, wanting to pull away, but his other arm snaked around her waist, forcing her tight against his hard body.

"Let me go," she begged.

"Oh, no, I can't let you go. I'm just getting started," he said in a horrible voice. He kneaded her stomach with his other hand.

Penny froze.

"See, I know it was you and your little friends who called the cops," he breathed, his mouth tickling her neck.

She squeezed her eyes shut.

"And messed up my car."

Penny blinked her eyes open and twisted her head around. Behind her was the cliff, and she felt the edge with the heel of her sandal, felt how it gave way, suddenly, to *emptiness*.

There was nowhere to go. He was going to kill her. Or worse. This was real, she thought. This was not one of her nightmares. They were going to find her dead, just like Mr. Cat. Or like that Jeffy kid. With all her fingers cut off.

Then she remembered the BB guns in the hollow tree just steps away. If she could just get to it and climb up into the branches, she could keep him away almost indefinitely with a steady stream of stinging pellets. But she had to get to the tree first.

Caleb whispered into her ear, "And I've been wondering why you've been trying to mess with me, Penny Carson."

And in that moment Penny did the only thing she could think of—she shoved her elbow hard into his stomach. He cursed, and when Penny felt his hands fall away from her waist, she leaped with all her might at a low-hanging branch of the tree. She grabbed on and tried to pull herself up, kicking out wildly when she felt Caleb reach for her legs, his hands tangling in her sandals and breaking one of the straps, and then there was nothing.

A soft thudding sound echoed through the woods.

Penny hung suspended from the tree for another minute, legs swinging, and then let go of the branch to fall to the dirt below. It seemed that her feet had barely touched the earth when the ground at the edge of the cliff gave way beneath her and she was falling, sliding down the slope on her stomach in a rain of loose, dry soil and pebbles. She groped the ground frantically, digging her fingers into the dirt until her nails broke, halting her descent by clutching at a thick exposed root. She held on to that root as tightly as she could, her feet scrambling to get a footing. And then something beneath her caught her eye, something far below, in the creek bed.

Something that looked an awful lot like Caleb.

Penny swallowed and clawed her way up the cliff, hand over hand. When she reached the top, her arms felt like rubber, and she fell to her knees, breathing hard. She stood up slowly, gingerly, her arm aching where Caleb had crushed it, and peered over the edge of the cliff.

Caleb's body lay facedown, blood streaming from somewhere under his head, his legs and arms spread out at unnatural angles.

There was a crackling, and the sky exploded above the woods from fireworks set off by some neighborhood kid. Was it a trick of the fading light, or did Caleb's hand just move?

Penny gave a ragged gasp and then turned and ran, the sound of buzzing cicadas rising around her like a roar, the green, thick place teeming with life.

· · ·

Penny was in the small blue bathroom upstairs. She had changed into shorts, an undershirt, and tennis shoes, her sandals ruined beyond repair now. She was inspecting the huge bruise on her arm from where Caleb had grabbed her, running her scratched and bleeding fingers lightly over it and wincing slightly. Her knees were scraped up and oozing blood from her slide down the cliff. She heard a small gasp and whirled around, startled, to see Teddy and Benji standing there.

"Where have you been?" Benji demanded, taking in her undershirt. "Thanks for sticking me with all the trash."

Penny shifted awkwardly and crossed her arms across her chest.

"You get the fireworks?" Benji asked.

Penny blanched. "Uh, no," she stammered.

Benji and Teddy exchanged glances.

"Some water had gotten into the tree and they were all ruined," Penny improvised.

"All of them?" Benji asked, aghast.

She nodded.

Benji exhaled. "That blows."

"What happened to you?" Teddy asked, eyeing the

angry-looking bruise on her arm, her scraped knees.

She tried to be nonchalant but failed, stammering, "I just, you know, fell. It was dark in the woods."

Teddy regarded his sister suspiciously.

Mrs. Albright called in through the front door, "Hey, you kids in here?"

"Upstairs, Mom!" Benji yelled.

"Didn't you hear me calling for you? We're leaving right now, so if you want to see the fireworks, you better get moving."

"We're coming," Benji yelled down.

"I gotta put on a shirt," Penny said.

"Hurry," Teddy said, shifting his weight on his crutches.

She met her brother's eyes in the mirror, gave a reassuring smile, and said calmly, like the big sister she was, "I'll be right down."

CHAPTER 13

She was running through the woods, the monster dogging her heels, his breath a hot lash against her neck. The moon was a thin shaft of light dancing between the trees, causing the shadows to move and waver and trick her eyes so that everything seemed farther away than it was. But still she ran, fast as she could, her sneakers silent on the soft, pine needle–carpeted floor.

There was a soft, plaintive meow behind her, and she knew instinctively that it was Mr. Cat. She turned to look back, and slammed right into a hard body, felt firm, steadying arms wrap around her.

"Hey. It's okay," the voice murmured soothingly.

She blinked up to see Caleb. He was wearing a black T-shirt, the thin fabric molding the lines of his chest so that she could see the curve of his collarbone.

He ran a hand down her hair, tucking a strand behind her ear.

"Nobody's going to hurt you," he whispered. "I'll take care of you."

She watched as he leaned toward her, his eyes near now. They were like the watchful eyes of a cat, and they were looking right at her, eating her up, as if she was the most beautiful girl he had ever seen. And maybe she was, because he was bending toward her, so close that she could smell the skin of his neck. It smelled hot, like fireworks, and she couldn't help herself, not with his warm arm around her back, his fingers toying with the hair at her neck—she just closed her eyes as his firm lips covered hers.

This was not the tentative kiss of a Benji—no, this was the assured kiss of a boy who knew what he wanted. The way he opened his mouth, and taunted her with the tip of his tongue, making lightning whip through her, causing her knees to buckle so that she clung to him. His will alone held her up.

His lips wandered to her neck, nuzzling the soft place behind her ear, but they suddenly felt cold, icy, and the little hairs on her arms stood up. She shivered and opened her eyes, squinting.

A dead rotting zombie Caleb grinned at her—

face bloated, lips blue, teeth blackened, skin rotting and peeling off in strips.

"*Penny,*" the zombie whispered, reaching for her.

She screamed.

And then Penny woke up, breathing hard.

Penny heard the familiar sounds of family life downstairs: Baby Sam bawling and her father's voice rumbling, and Teddy yelling that he couldn't find his Super Ball, the brand new fluorescent yellow one, and had the dumb baby eaten it? It was all so perfectly normal, normal in a way that felt disconnected to Penny, as if the rest of the world was moving right along while she watched from the sidelines.

"Penny! Breakfast!" her mother called.

Penny sighed and swung her feet over the bed. She felt hot and sticky, and just a little feverish.

In the mirror on the closet door, she studied her limp dirty-blond hair, her sunburned cheeks, the slender way her neck rose above her shoulders, almost pretty if she looked a certain way. She remembered Caleb nuzzling that place on her neck and shook her head, startled. Better, she thought harshly, to look at the bruise on her arm where he had grabbed her, the bruise that was fading now, gone a yellowish-purple.

Nearly a week had passed since that single heart-stopping moment on the cliff with Caleb, a moment that had changed her life forever.

"Penny, I'm not going to call you again!" her mother hollered, exasperation plain in her voice.

"Coming!" Penny called back, padding across the carpet to find her slippers. For a brief moment her eye was drawn back to the mirror, and that was when she saw him: the dark angry boy, all bloody and full of fury, just waiting to reach out from behind the glass and hurt her bad, make her pay, finish the job this time.

She gasped in shock, tripping back and banging into the small side table with the porcelain lamp that had been a present from Nana. The lamp teetered and fell and Penny lunged for it, catching it before it hit the floor. She looked back at the mirror fearfully, brandishing the lamp like a weapon in front of her.

But he was gone.

"Let's go," Mac muttered to himself, leg twitching. He wore a thick bandage on his cheek, a souvenir from the bat bite. He'd gotten four stitches, and Penny's dad said that he'd probably have a scar.

"Shut up, Mad Dog," Benji teased. The boys had

taken to calling Mac "Mad Dog" when they'd heard about the rabies shots Mac also had to have.

"How long does it take to put on a swimsuit?" Oren demanded, his face looking drawn. Oren had fared better than Mac from his trip to the emergency room on the Fourth. Since he'd thrown up nearly everything he'd eaten by the time he reached the hospital, all he'd gotten was a shot, and then he'd been sent home to spend the next two days in bed, where he threw up some more. He'd lost a few pounds, and Penny figured he wouldn't be eating clams again anytime soon.

"It's not fair," Teddy said, banging his crutches irritably. "I want to go in the water. I don't wanna sit around and watch. Who cares if my stupid cast gets wet?"

"But if your cast gets wet, it'll melt," Oren said.

"And smell," Mac added.

"It already smells," Teddy muttered.

The voices swirled around Penny, but it was like she wasn't even there. She was just going through the motions. Putting on a swimsuit and flip-flops. Sitting on the front porch and waiting for her mother to drive them over to the public pool. She didn't know how she was supposed to be excited to go swimming when all she could think about was Caleb.

Everything had changed. She had gone through some door and there was no going back. It was like she had been sleepwalking before, and finally she was awake and everything was brighter somehow, the colors sharper. Even the blacktop driveway radiating heat in thick waves reminded her of the hot, stinging touch of Caleb's skin on hers, the tar smell of his fingers gripping her arms.

"Hey," Mac said, nodding toward the Bukvics' house. "You seen *him* over there lately?"

"Uh, no," Penny said with forced casualness. "Maybe, they're, like, fighting or something," she improvised, amazed at how calm she sounded. She added a careless shrug for good measure.

Becky Albright came running up the block wearing a pink gingham bathing suit and carrying a towel and inflatable floaties. She looked waifish from her bout with food poisoning.

The sight of the little girl, so innocent, rubbed against Penny like a sliver digging its way under her fingernail.

"Get lost, Becky," she said sharply.

Becky looked startled, tears welling up in her eyes. "But Mom said I could come," she said, her voice trembling with hurt.

It was on the tip of Penny's tongue to say that she couldn't care less when she realized that all the boys were staring at her with strange looks on their faces. And then Mrs. Carson walked out the front door, Baby Sam on her hip.

"You kids ready?" her mother asked brightly, her own sleek bikini clearly visible beneath her cover-up.

Penny sat sandwiched between Benji and Oren in the backseat of the minivan. Their combined boyish scents of dirty sneakers and sunscreen lotion attacked her senses. It was all she could do to close her eyes and feign sleep when she was penned in by the warmth of their bare skin pressing against her. Oren's curly hair tickled her shoulder, but she held herself still, even when the minivan hit a bump and Benji reached out to steady himself, his elbow glancing off her chest.

It was with relief that Penny dove into the deep end to cool off all the hot sensations thrumming through her body. She held her breath as she glided across the length of the pool, remembering how she had swum in the creek mere weeks ago. Could she ever swim there again, knowing that Caleb's blood had soaked into the rocky creek bed?

She broke the surface, opening her eyes and then

shutting them reflexively, the sharp chlorine stinging. She gasped.

"Are they trying to blind us?" Mac exclaimed, rubbing his eyes.

"They must have just put chlorine in the pool," Oren said, blinking rapidly.

Penny rubbed uselessly at her eyes, trying to rub away the stinging. She opened her eyes a crack, but everything was hazy.

The kids paddled to the side of the pool and clung to the edge.

"Let's play Marco Polo," Benji said.

"Yeah," Zachary agreed. "There are a ton of kids here today."

"Yo, anyone who wants to play Marco Polo, head over here!" Mac yelled.

"I do!" Becky Albright said eagerly.

"Of course she does," Penny said sourly, earning a look from Benji.

The slim, pretty lifeguard who was sitting on a tall chair shouted: "No Fish Out of Water, got it?"

Fish Out of Water was when you snuck out of the pool, ran around, and leaped back in before the person who was It shouted "Fish Out of Water." Sometimes kids took terrible spills when they were

Fish Out of Water, slipping on wet tiles.

Mac groaned. "Come on."

"No way," the lifeguard said, with a firm shake of her shining shoulder-length hair. "You stay in the pool or you're out of here, got it?"

"I'll be It," Penny volunteered, squinting. Her eyes hurt so much from the chlorine that she didn't much care if she had to be the one to swim around blind.

"Okay," Mac agreed.

Penny closed her eyes and waded in a slow circle, counting to ten in a loud voice. She heard the anxious giggle of the other kids as they rushed to get away from her. Penny paddled around aimlessly, her feet kicking at the water. "Marco!" she called.

"Polo!" the voices echoed back at her.

She felt the kids swarming around her, brushing her thighs, her rear end. Someone grabbed her kneecap and she reached for him, but he swam away, her hands catching nothing but water. She circled warily, calling out "Marco!" and trying to gauge the distance by the sound of the shouts coming back to her. Kids shouted "Polo!" but they were farther away now, maybe even at the other end of the pool. She heard Mac and Benji talking to the pretty lifeguard.

"You're sixteen?" Mac asked in an impressed-sounding voice.

"Just last month," the lifeguard replied silkily.

"So, you must be like a really good swimmer, huh?" Mac asked, sounding incredibly awkward to Penny's ear.

Voices came and went, rising around her and then disappearing as the taunting kids swam away. One voice—was it Oren's?—seemed to stick in her head, and she swam toward it, into the deep end. She could tell it was the deep end by the way her feet could feel nothing, even when she bounced down toward the bottom. She must be at the very deepest part of the pool, she thought, and then there was that voice again.

"Polo!"

"Marco!" she called, feeling certain that she was nearly on top of him now.

"Polo!"

She lunged, but all she grasped was water. Frustrated, she paddled around, trying to catch her breath, her feet kicking in a rhythmic motion, and felt someone brush her thigh.

"Marco!" she shouted.

A hand snaked around her ankle.

"Hey," she said.

Suddenly, without any warning, firm hands gripped both her ankles and she was pulled beneath the water. She tried to kick out, but it was useless. Flailing in fear, panic roaring in her ears, she was pulled relentlessly down by the hard hands. She needed to take a breath but couldn't; her lungs were freezing up. Someone was trying to drown her!

Still underwater, Penny opened her eyes, the chlorine stinging them brutally. She looked down, and for a moment she saw a ghostly face, strangely distorted in the dark, watery depth of the pool. *But it couldn't be!* she thought wildly.

Caleb.

Then everything went black.

When Penny came to, she was lying on the hard tiles, her mother's nose just inches away from her own. And then she was coughing and spitting up what felt like gallons of water. Someone turned her on her side, and the water kept coming.

"Thank heavens!" her mother said with a sigh, leaning back on her ankles.

Penny's eyes fluttered open, her tongue sharp with the metallic aftertaste of chlorine. The boys were jostling one another to get to her, and the pretty lifeguard was leaning over.

"Give her some room," her mother ordered.

"Caleb!" Penny sputtered, her slender body racked with the force of her coughs.

"What?" her mother asked, startled.

"It was Caleb!"

Her mom looked at Oren, alarmed. "Did you see Caleb? Did you see him in the pool?"

"No way, Mrs. Carson. And I know what he looks like," he said in a solemn voice.

"Oren saved you, Penny!" Teddy blurted out.

"Thanks," she whispered hoarsely, meeting Oren's eyes. He blushed.

"Any of you kids see Caleb?"

They all shook their heads in bewilderment.

"Honey," her mother said, smoothing Penny's hair back in a soothing gesture. "Are you sure you saw him? None of the other kids saw him, and I was watching, too."

"But I saw him," Penny began, her lower lip trembling.

"We didn't see him, Penny," Benji said. "And he's pretty hard to miss."

Penny looked at the shocked faces of the boys, the

worried expression on her mom's face, and wondered if she was losing her mind.

"I . . . I don't know," she stuttered. And then the stress of the past week came crashing down on her and she burst into tears.

Penny looked out dully at the passing landscape as her mother drove them home, the other kids quiet. The minivan pulled into the familiar driveway on Mockingbird Lane, and the boys jumped out, towels in tow.

"See you tomorrow, Penny," Benji said in a subdued voice.

"Yeah, see you, Penny," Oren echoed. Penny suddenly realized how tall he was, his arms ropy with muscles. He had to be pretty strong to have pulled her out of the pool by himself. How had she never noticed this before?

"Let's get inside, you two," her mom said to Penny and Teddy, hoisting up the baby. "Penny, I want you to take a hot shower, okay?"

"Okay," she said.

It would take a lot more than a hot shower to make things right, Penny knew. A hot shower would not get rid of the guilt that taunted her. Had she kicked Caleb over the cliff edge when he'd grabbed at her feet, or had the ground simply given way? And worse, had he still been alive when she'd left him there? But nobody could survive a fall that high . . . could they?

Had his hand moved?

Maybe, she thought, a shiver running through her, his ghost was after her. She remembered something Nana had told her long ago, about how restless spirits sometimes roamed the earth searching for vengeance. Was Caleb a restless spirit? The face in the pool had been hazy, but it had looked so much like him. She didn't know anymore. She felt like she was going crazy.

Penny went up to her bedroom. She stripped off her shorts, kicked off her flip-flops, and stood there in her damp, chlorine-scented swimsuit. She looked at the shorts, lying there in a tangle, and suddenly knew what to do.

She would call Nana.

She thought of the stuffy little pantry in the kitchen in Key West where Nana kept all sorts of odd-colored bottles, full of sand and seashells. Her spells, she called them.

Maybe one strong enough to get rid of a vengeful ghost.

Penny waited until her parents were in bed and then crept downstairs and flicked on the small lamp by the phone, the warm yellow light glowing comfortingly in the dark kitchen. She dialed the number by heart. Nana picked up on the second ring.

"Hello?" the familiar husky voice said, and Penny almost wept in relief.

She curled herself up on the chair and whispered in an urgent voice, "It's me, Nana. It's me, Penny."

"Hello, Penny dear. How nice to hear from my favorite granddaughter." Her voice crackled across the distance. "How is your baby brother doing?"

"Fine."

"And your mother and father?"

"Fine."

"Teddy?"

"Fine."

"So you're the only one who's not fine, I'm guessing."

"Uh-huh."

"Tell me," Nana said in a calm voice. Penny could

almost see her in the sweet little kitchen, a cup of tea within easy reach, the scent of lemon in the air.

Penny gripped the phone. "Someone tried to drown me today."

There was a distinct pause, and then Nana said in a sharp voice, "Tried to drown you?"

"This boy Caleb," she whispered.

"Go on."

"Except I think it was his ghost who tried to drown me."

"What do you mean, 'his ghost'?"

Penny felt it building in her, the aching need to tell someone what had happened, to share this terrible burden.

"There was this accident—"

The kitchen light suddenly flicked on, and her mother was standing there in her nightgown, an annoyed expression on her face.

"Who are you talking to at this hour? You're supposed to be in bed. It's past midnight."

Penny gulped. "Nana," she whispered.

Her mother's features softened, and she walked over and took the phone from Penny. "Go to bed," she ordered in a firm voice.

Penny ran out of the kitchen, and then paused in the hallway to listen to her mother.

"I'm sorry, Mom," her mother said in a tired voice. "It's been a bad day. We had a scare at the pool. I'll call you tomorrow and tell you about it, okay? Penny's just a little overwrought right now."

CHAPTER 14

The day was relentlessly hot, even deep in the cool of the woods. A stingy breeze stirred the trees, carrying the faint scent of something rotting, and Caleb's face rose before Penny's eyes, hard and angry.

Several days had passed since the incident at the pool, and with each passing day, Penny's fear grew. It didn't help matters any that she felt like she was being watched, stalked by a predator just out of sight, behind that innocent-looking row of bushes, or crouched in the shadows of the garage.

Only the day before, she and the boys had witnessed Amy Bukvic stomp down the block and bang on the Devlins' front door, looking for her boyfriend.

"Maybe he dumped her," Mac guffawed, watching as Amy practically ran up the block in tears after a terse exchange with a gray-looking Mr. Devlin.

What had Mr. Devlin said to Amy? Did he think Caleb had just taken off, business as usual, or did he suspect foul play? And if Mr. Devlin thought his son was dead, where were the police? Were they the ones hiding in the shadows, waiting for just the right moment to jump out and slap the handcuffs on her?

Or—and this thought shook her like nothing else could—was Mr. Devlin secretly nursing his son back to health behind the drawn blinds of the house? Or maybe it was Caleb out there, hiding somewhere in the silky dark tangle of the woods. A zombie, or worse: *alive* and really pissed off at her—

"Yo Penny, wake up!" Mac was hollering angrily, as a box of nails flew past her, spilling everywhere.

"*You* wake up!" she shot back.

Penny didn't even want to be here in the woods with the boys, building another stupid fort. She didn't know what she wanted anymore, but she knew it was not *this*. It all seemed so childish to her now, so silly.

"What did you say?" Mac said slowly.

"Chill out, Mac," Benji said, defending her. "You're just mad 'cause of your mom."

Teddy's ears pricked up. "What about your mom?"

"She's acting all weird," Mac said, mouth twitching. "She's gonna send me down to my stupid grandmother's in Georgia."

"Because of Caleb?" Teddy asked. Mac and Oren had carried Teddy down to the woods because he couldn't maneuver on the uneven ground with his crutches. He sat on a log and spent a lot of time supervising the other boys.

Mac nodded. "At the beginning of August. She said the fire was the last straw."

"That blows," Oren said with a low whistle.

And then Mac said, "Your bratty sister's here, Benji."

Becky Albright stood in the clearing, her crisp white cotton eyelet dress out of place in the cool green woods. She seemed to glow where she stood.

"How'd you find us?" Benji demanded.

Becky shook her head, refusing to tell.

"If Mom finds out you came here, she'll kill me. Go home."

"No!"

Benji marched up and grabbed her arm. "Then I'll take you myself."

Becky started shrieking her head off. Benji glared at her in exasperation, and Penny walked over and competently took Becky's hand. "Shut up."

Becky was so startled by Penny's sharp tone that she did just that.

"I'll take her back," Penny said, happy to get away from the creek.

"Thanks," Benji called in a grateful voice.

Becky followed Penny quietly. They were halfway out of the woods when Becky stopped dead in her tracks.

"I want to go back!" the little girl declared petulantly, and for a brief moment some part of Penny wanted to slap that defiant little face, slap it hard.

"Too bad," Penny said sharply. "I don't have time to waste on bratty little girls." She grabbed Becky's wrist and pulled the resisting child after her.

"Why are you being so mean to me?" Becky cried out.

"I don't know what you're talking about," Penny said.

Penny stood in her driveway beneath the rapidly darkening sky, watching the porch lights flick on up and down the block, casting small pools of light. Down at the cul-de-sac, kids were gathering for flashlight tag.

She had taken great care with her appearance this evening. She was wearing a pair of skimpy jean shorts and one of her mother's skinny tank tops, a racy red one that entwined her body like a pair of hands. And she had put on the bra, thrilling at the way it made her chest curve softly beneath the thin fabric. This outfit made her feel different, wilder, like she was a cat that had just figured out how to climb trees.

Across the street, Amy was sitting on the step of her front porch, applying nail polish to her toenails.

With a careless ease she had not suspected she possessed, Penny walked across the short length of asphalt, one step after another, and right up to Amy.

Amy's eyes widened slightly as she took in Penny's appearance, pausing on the tank top. Something approaching grudging admiration flickered in her eyes briefly and then disappeared.

"Hey," Penny said, sitting down casually next to Amy.

Amy ignored her, expertly applying the bright red nail polish. Her face was splotchy, as if she'd been crying.

Penny looked at Amy's handiwork. "Nice color."

Amy narrowed her eyes, and Penny could almost see the biting reply on the tip of her tongue. And then Amy said, "Thanks."

"Can I borrow it sometime?"

Amy shrugged.

From the cul-de-sac, Benji's voice rang loudly. "Come on, Penny! We're picking sides now."

Penny hesitated. Amy stared at her challengingly.

Something had changed. She didn't want to play flashlight tag. Well, part of her did, but another part of her just wanted to sit here and put on nail polish and let the warm night air wash over her bare skin and talk about how it felt to have a boy like Caleb kiss your neck.

"Penny!"

Penny shook herself. Who was this girl inhabiting her body? What was she doing, sitting here with Amy and thinking about kissing boys? She stood up quickly, shaken.

"See ya," she said, and rushed down the block, leaving Amy to stare after her.

Mac laid down the rules. "Okay, no hiding in garages, and the top of the storm drain is jail. Let's pick sides."

Mac and Benji started the slow process of picking teams. There were over twenty kids. Mac picked Oren. Benji picked Penny. Mac picked Billy Gimble. Benji picked Alex Knief. Mac picked Ralphie Kearns. Benji picked Simon Hamel. This went on until there were only two kids left. Poor Teddy was relegated to sitting in the cul-de-sac, watching the action.

Mac eyed the last two kids. Stan McCann and Zachary Evreth. A lame choice either way.

"I'll take Stan and you get Zachary," Mac finally said to Benji, his eyes lingering on Zachary with obvious distaste.

"Hey, Penny," Zachary said shyly, coming over to Benji's side.

Penny smiled back.

It was barely light now. By the time the game started, it would be pitch-black.

Mac nodded at Benji. "Toss to see who goes first?"

Benji dug a quarter out of his pocket and flipped. "Heads," he called.

The bright quarter landed tails up in his hand.

Mac looked at his team and nodded. "Let's go."

Penny and her teammates waited ten minutes and then took off into the dark, their flashlights scanning bushes, sides of houses, dark alcoves. Fireflies blinked in and out of the darkness. Every once in a while Penny saw a kid on her own team dart by, flashlight shining. She gave a quick flash back in support.

In short order her team had caught five of the ten

kids. Since they were limited to front and back yards, many of the hiding places were well known. Penny tried to get into the spirit of the game, but her heart just wasn't in it. And for the first time in her life, she felt scared to be outside in the dark. She kept hearing soft meows and lingering barks, as if the ghosts of the pets Caleb had killed were following her in the dark, eyes glowing.

Her flashlight abruptly winked off.

"Darn," she said.

A hand touched her on the shoulder and she whirled around, heart pounding, flashlight raised high to protect her.

"Hey," Zachary said, a confused look on his shiny face. He flicked his flashlight on and shone it up at his face. "We're on the same team."

Penny slowly expelled her indrawn breath, lowering the flashlight. "You scared me," she said.

"Sorry," he replied, looking crestfallen.

"It's okay. I'm just a little jumpy."

"Because of what happened at the pool?"

She nodded.

He looked at her flashlight. "Batteries?"

"I think it's broken."

His face brightened. "We can both use mine."

"Okay," she said, unaccountably relieved. She actually felt a little better being with another person.

"Want a piece of gum?" he asked.

"Where do you get all your gum?" she asked, taking a piece.

He winked at her like he was letting her in on a big secret. "Baseball cards."

"I have a pretty good idea where Oren is," Penny said. She had overheard Teddy whispering to Oren about the storm drain, how it was a good place to hide.

Zachary handed Penny the flashlight. "Lead the way."

The secret of flashlight tag was in the surprise, Penny knew. If someone who was hiding saw your flashlight coming, it was easy for them to take off to a new hiding place. So the best thing to do was to creep along quietly in the dark, flicking your flashlight on at the last moment.

Zachary stepped on a twig with a loud crunch.

"Shhh," she urged.

"Where are we going?" he whispered.

"The storm drain."

He blanched. "By Devlins'?"

"It's pretty far from the house," she said reassuringly.

Penny crept quietly through the outskirts of the woods to the yawning, snakelike storm drainpipe. She eased herself up into the opening and knelt on the rusty corrugated metal.

"Tag!" she shouted, aiming Zachary's flashlight down the pipe and flicking it on.

Zachary jostled behind her to get a look.

But it wasn't Oren after all. It was Becky. Her back was turned to them, and her gold hair glinted in the darkness.

"Come on, Becky," Penny said. "We got you fair and square."

But Becky just crouched there, ignoring them, as if they would go away if she waited long enough.

"Benji's right," Penny muttered to herself. Becky could be such a brat.

Penny crawled the rest of the way down the pipe, the light from the flashlight bobbing.

The little girl seemed so still.

Too still.

Mr. Cat's stuffed body flashed through her mind.

"Becky!" she shouted.

Penny scrambled down into the storm drain and grabbed Becky by the shoulder. Becky's body flopped like a doll and fell onto Penny. The little girl's eyes were wide and glassy, her neck a streak of red.

Zachary made a strange choking sound, turned away, and started retching.

The flashlight swept across the wall, and that was when Penny saw the lightning bolt—freshly drawn with chalk—pointing down at Becky's dead body.

CHAPTER 15

She just had to go and look, to see for herself.

As she descended the cliff to the creek bed in the still morning air, Penny remembered how ambulances and police cars had filled Mockingbird Lane after Becky had been found, how it had seemed that the street was one great flashing light. The still night had been filled with the screams of Mrs. Albright, and Mr. Albright had had to be forcibly restrained by the police after he threatened to go over and kill Caleb himself. Penny hadn't had the courage to tell him that he didn't have to bother.

She smelled him before she saw him, and she gagged. It was a smell so incredible, so horrible, that she knew she would never forget it, not ever. It smelled like that dead frog, but a hundred times worse. The smell of hot, rotting meat.

Caleb's body lay sprawled like a broken puppet that had had its strings cut, arms flopping forward. Old rubber tires, rusty aluminum cans, and ancient sneakers littered the dry creek bed, and the dead body seemed to fit there, oddly enough, as if the woods had taken back one of its own.

The body was black and puffy, bloated from being out in the sun. Ants crawled over it in determined little lines, winding their way over arms and across the nape of Caleb's neck, as if he was one big scrap of toast with jelly. Some animal had been at him, and his clothes were bitten away in places.

But it was his hand, in the end, that got Penny— the way the fingers were splayed out, reaching forward, leaving long furrows scratched in the dirt, as if he'd been trying to crawl away.

She stumbled back and threw up until there was nothing left in her stomach, then tucked her head between her knees, feeling light-headed and breathing hard.

Somewhere in the back of her head she'd worried that Caleb was still alive, or maybe even a zombie, wandering around killing little girls and stuffing them into storm drains. But looking at the body now, for the first time since that horrible day, she knew for a fact that it hadn't been Caleb who had killed Becky last night. No, he had been too busy lying in the creek being dead.

She couldn't deny it anymore.

It had been someone else all along. Someone who wanted them all to think it was Caleb. Someone who knew Caleb's history and how everyone would react when things started up again.

A shaft of sun broke through the thick trees and struck the dry creek bed. Something bright glittered.

Penny got up and went over to investigate. It was Caleb's silver cigarette case, fallen from his pocket. She picked it up gingerly and forced herself to open it, expecting, even now, to see a row of crusty, dried-up pinky fingers.

Three stale cigarettes tumbled out.

She pocketed the case and ran through the woods, the heavy weight of it burning her like a hot coal.

They met in the musty quiet of Mac's basement to speak of the unspeakable.

Benji looked positively gray. It had been two days since Becky's body had been found, and he had aged in that short time. Gone were the impish lines around his mouth, the ones that made him look as if he might burst into a grin at any moment. His mouth was a grim, hard line, his eyes dull. He seemed a ghost of the boy who had kissed her in the cool, damp woods.

"How's your mom and dad?" Penny asked gently.

"Mom's sort of messed up. She won't come out of her room. Mrs. Schuyler's helping out with the cooking and stuff," Benji said, the pale evening light filtering through a crack of basement window.

Penny could only imagine how he felt. He was Becky's brother, he was supposed to be looking out for her. What if it had been Teddy?

"The funeral's gonna be tomorrow," Benji added in a hollow voice.

Oren shook his head. "Did the police arrest Caleb?"

"They went to question him last night, but he wasn't home," Benji said. "His parents say he hasn't been home for days."

Since the Fourth, Penny wanted to blurt out, but bit down on her tongue so hard she tasted blood.

"He took off," Mac said, stating the obvious. "He's a million miles away by now. The police are still looking for him, right?"

Benji nodded.

"So now what?" Zachary asked anxiously. Zachary had been particularly shaken up during the last few days, as if he was just waiting for Caleb to finish him off, too. Part of Penny wanted to tell him that he didn't ever have to worry about being beaten up by Caleb again.

"What do you mean, 'now what'?" Benji was angry, angrier than they had ever seen him.

There was a flurry of noise upstairs. From the sharp click-clack of shoes, they knew it was the moms.

"This way," Mac hissed, getting up and walking through a door that led to the unfinished part of the basement, where the floor was poured cement and it smelled mildewy because it flooded every spring. Mac pointed silently to a grate in the ceiling.

"What are we doing?" Zachary blurted.

"Shut up, you retard!" Mac shot back in a fierce whisper, punching Zachary hard in the arm.

"Ow!" Zachary winced, rubbing his arm and flinching as Mac raised his fist again.

Voices from the kitchen above drifted down, strong and clear.

"Have they found him?" Penny heard her mom say, in a voice tinged with worry.

"No," Mrs. Bukvic said angrily. "They'll never find him. He's gone. He killed Buster, too, I just know it."

"We have to keep the kids indoors," one of the mothers declared.

Mrs. McHale groaned. "All summer? That'll kill *me*!"

"Maybe if we just keep them in the yards. . . ." This from her mother.

"I tell you, we can't take any chances, not with him on the street."

"Bethany, could Phil come over and take a look at the locks on our doors and make sure they're okay?" Mrs. Loew asked nervously. "I worry, being alone and—"

"Of course," her mother murmured back.

This was how it had all started in the first place, Penny thought. They had let fear and panic and, most of all, the seductive voices of the adults convince them that it was Caleb. She could see it clearly now, how she had allowed her fears to sweep her along, like a leaf in the water, to the easy, obvious conclusion that Caleb was the culprit because he was a bad boy from a strange family who didn't quite fit in.

If she could only go back to that one moment when she was standing on the edge of the cliff, look-ing down at the creek, she would. Because now, deep in her soul, she knew Caleb had still been alive—in her mind's eye she could see his hand shudder, reaching forward. And she had left him there to die, alone and in the dark. Didn't that make her just as bad as Becky's killer?

She looked across the dark basement at Benji, his face a mask of grief. Nothing in this world would bring his sister back. Penny felt a swirl of self-hatred at how mean she had been to the little girl the last time she'd seen her, but still she couldn't bear to let Caleb take the blame for Becky, not when the real killer was still out there somewhere.

"You guys," she said tentatively. "What if it was someone else? You know, like the policeman said: who else knew that we were playing flashlight tag?"

Mac exploded. "What are you talking about?"

"*You've* been the one all along who's been saying that Caleb's after us. What about Teddy?" Oren asked.

"Yeah, what about me?" Teddy said, stricken. "I told you it was Caleb!"

"It's just that I don't think he killed Becky," Penny said in an awkward rush. "I mean, why would he do it?"

Benji walked right up to her, a terrible expression on his face. "Because he's evil, Penny," he said in a voice so hard she almost flinched. "Got it?"

She looked at the coldly furious faces, and she got it all right. It was just like Mr. Schuyler always said.

The only person you could count on was yourself.

Penny sat quietly in the pew.

It was a huge church, bigger than the one she and her family occasionally attended. The ceiling arched high, and the walls had lots of ornate stained glass depicting the life of Jesus: Jesus in the Garden of Gethsemane, Jesus and the apostles at the Last Supper, Jesus suspended on the cross. Jesus' eyes seemed dark and cool and condemning. A little like Caleb's eyes, Penny thought with a shiver.

Teddy sat next to her, stiff and uncomfortable in his suit jacket and tie. He was wearing sweatpants, and his cast poked out of it, a dark reminder to Penny of all that had happened.

Farther down in the pew were her dad and mom, and Baby Sam. Penny swung her shiny black patent-leather shoes back and forth, thinking hard. She remembered how the police had questioned her and the other kids after Becky's body had been found. How they had kept asking her the same questions over and over. *Had she seen any strangers in the neighborhood? Or any big kids she didn't recognize? What about odd-looking cars?*

Her own parents had lectured her and Teddy in the car on the way to church.

"You two are to keep your eyes open from now on," her mother said, a fierce look on her face. "If you see Caleb, you are to run to the nearest house immediately. Do you understand? He's killed a little girl. There's no telling what he'll do next."

They had nodded mutely back. Penny knew the other kids had all received similar lectures from their parents.

It was obvious to Penny that with everyone looking for Caleb, the real killer would be off guard, careless. She had to find him before everyone discovered that Caleb was dead. Her gaze swept the church.

He could be right here, she thought slowly.

Penny craned her neck to look through the crowd. There was Zachary and his mom, way up front. Zachary's mom was wailing away like a professional mourner, and it struck Penny as odd. Had Mrs. Evreth even known Becky? And wasn't there something just a bit creepy about the way she was always trying to lure the kids to her "Bible group"? Mrs. Evreth wailed loudly, and with each loud sob an embarrassed-looking Zachary seemed to sink lower in his seat. Penny felt sorry for him.

She spotted Oren and his mom. Oren's dad was sitting on the other side of the aisle with his new girlfriend. Oren sat very still, his curly hair tamed, his suit pressed. Oren was very smart, she knew, the smartest of them all when it came to school and grades. He always got straight A's. He was an easy kid to play with, fair and reasonable. But he had also been acting strange lately, sort of angry and withdrawn, something that she had chalked up to his parents getting divorced. But maybe there was more to it.

Mac, wearing a dark, tight-fitting suit and a belligerent expression, sat hunched over in front of Oren and kept turning around to whisper to him, clearly bored by the proceedings. Penny thought of all the times that Mac had dismissed her fears. Also, he had always hated Becky the most. As if sensing that Penny was studying him, Mac turned around and stared at her, his face hard.

Penny's swinging feet banged into the pew ahead in nervous excitement.

"Penny!" her mother hissed, a look of displeasure on her face. "Settle down."

Penny looked down, chastened. But when she looked up, Mac was still staring at her.

■ ■ ■

The next morning, as Penny walked down the street toward the cul-de-sac, a police car drove by, moving slowly down Mockingbird Lane. There had been a lot of this lately, a lot of police cars and policemen wandering about the streets, watching and looking and, Penny rather hoped, protecting.

"Hey, Penny! How ya doing?"

Her head whipped around. It was old Mr. Schuyler. He was sitting on his front porch, wearing a pair of faded overalls and drinking a beer.

"Hi, Mr. Schuyler," she said, walking up to the porch.

"Sure is hot," he said. A lopsided little smile wreathed his red face.

"Sure is," she agreed.

"You want to go to Wallaby Farms tonight?"

"That'd be great," Penny said with a bright smile, thinking, *Why is this old guy always doing stuff for us? Always organizing softball competitions and taking us for ice cream?* And that look he'd given her a minute ago. It had seemed just a bit, well, weird.

He rocked back in his chair, and Penny noticed a number of empties lined up at his feet. "Come on down after dinner, all right?"

"You bet," she said. "And I'll bring the boys."

"Of course, of course. Bring the boys." Had his smile slipped for a second?

Penny walked across the cul-de-sac and flopped down on the curb next to Teddy, Mac, Oren, and Zachary. The sun was hot and the air tangy with the scent of fresh-cut grass.

"Where've you been?" Oren asked, looking up from his task. He was zapping ants with Mac's new magnifying glass.

Mac said, "Here, let me do the worm."

Penny shrugged. "Around."

Benji was absent. Penny had gone over earlier that day to see if he wanted to play, but he had merely shaken his head when he answered the door, the sound of his mother's weeping loud in the background.

Penny relaxed back on her elbows, looking over at Mr. Schuyler. "Do you guys think that Mr. Schuyler's weird? The way he hates the government and the police and all?"

"I hate the police," Mac muttered.

"What do you mean by 'weird'?" Oren asked.

"You know, always doing stuff, buying us ice cream," Penny explained.

"I like ice cream," Teddy said.

"Me, too," Zachary said. From his bulging belly, Penny had no doubt that Zachary liked ice cream.

"Yeah, but don't you think it's kind of odd that he spends money on us?" she persisted.

"No," Teddy said quickly, like Penny was going to screw everything up for them.

But Oren saw where she was going. "But they don't have any kids. That's why he does it. We're, like, his . . . I don't know, grandkids or something."

"Don't question a good thing," said Mac, who was frying a long, plump worm. It sizzled. "If he wants to spend his money on us, let him."

"Yeah, let him," Teddy seconded, waving a crutch in the air.

The next morning, Penny headed over to the Schuylers'. Mr. Schuyler was fast asleep on the front porch, snoring away.

The trip to Wallaby Farms the previous night had not been very much fun. Everyone was still freaked out about Becky, and Mr. and Mrs. Albright wouldn't let Benji go.

Penny knocked gently on the screen door, and Mrs. Schuyler opened it, all smiles.

"Penny, dear!" she said, wiping her hands on her apron. Mrs. Schuyler was wearing a flower-print dress, the kind grandmothers usually wore, and a nice fragrance rose from her, the smell of flour and melted butter.

"Hi, Mrs. Schuyler."

The elderly woman took a long look at her dozing husband.

"Why don't you come in so we don't wake him up? He needs his beauty sleep," Mrs. Schuyler said, holding open the door and ushering her into the cool of the house. "I'm afraid you caught me in the middle of baking," she added.

"That's okay," Penny said easily. "What are you making?"

"My famous gingerbread." Mrs. Schuyler smiled.

"I love your gingerbread," Penny declared, following her into the kitchen. The kitchen counter was strewn with tin pans and ingredients: flour, sugar, eggs.

"Why don't you sit there while I finish, and when it's baking, we can go out back and have some lemonade. How does that sound?" Mrs. Schuyler asked.

It sounded pretty good to Penny, especially the lemonade part. "Okay."

Penny sat on a high antique stool while Mrs. Schuyler kept up a steady stream of conversation, telling Penny how she had learned this recipe when she was at her mother's knees; it was her grandmother's recipe, and the secret ingredient was nutmeg.

"Nutmeg," Penny said, looking around, seeing with new eyes the kitchen she had been in a million times. It was a very old-fashioned kitchen, with hanging pots and dried herbs suspended from hooks in the ceiling.

"Will you be okay?"

Penny snapped her head back to look at Mrs. Schuyler. The old woman was taking off her apron. "What?"

"I've run out of cinnamon. I'm just going to run next door. Will you be okay here on your own?"

Would she be okay? You bet she would. "Sure," she said.

Mrs. Schuyler smiled. "I won't be a moment."

A moment was long enough.

"Okay," Penny said with a cheery smile as the woman disappeared out the front door.

Penny waited until she heard the door slam and then ran to the den, pausing to glance out the front window to make sure Mr. Schuyler was still asleep. He was.

The den sported a worn-looking Barcalounger and old, dark furniture—big, heavy, masculine pieces. A desk was set against the wall, with a big chair pulled up to it. Probably Mr. Schuyler's. She quickly rummaged through the drawers, her heart pounding fast. The top drawer contained lots of scraps of paper— ancient receipts from the look of it, all for feed. And a list that said "Hogs Slaughtered," with the year, weight, and name of each pig neatly written out: Jack Daniel, Old Rye, Brandy, Tom Collins. What was with the weird names? Why would you name a pig Old Rye? Pigs should be named Porky or Curly Tail. She hadn't even known that Mr. Schuyler had been a pig farmer; she thought he'd grown corn, or hay, or something involving fields and tractors.

Penny rifled through the bottom drawer. It was stuffed with tattered copies of *The Old Farmer's Almanac*. She paused when she reached the bottom of the stack, her eyes widening. The naked girl on the front of the magazine winked up at Penny. Penny had seen girly magazines before—the boys had kept an ancient one at the fort—but this one was something else. Penny paged through it and then slapped the magazine shut and closed the drawer quickly, looking behind her.

Mr. Schuyler was right on the front porch! What if he came in for a beer and found her snooping through his desk?

In the corner of the room stood a tall, dark oak cabinet with an old-fashioned key in the lock. Penny turned the key and the door popped open. She drew a breath.

Row after row of gleaming guns blinked out at her. Long, black-barreled rifles; shotguns; sleek black handguns; an old ivory-handled pistol; deadly-looking arrows; and a scary-looking bow. There were boxes and boxes of bullets and a pair of binoculars . . . and thick hunting knives.

"Penny!"

Penny whirled around and shut the door to the cabinet quickly. Mrs. Schuyler was standing there, holding a container of cinnamon, a puzzled look on her kind face. "You weren't looking in that cabinet, were you?"

"Uh, no," Penny stammered.

Mrs. Schuyler walked over and locked the cabinet, slipping the key into the pocket of her dress. "I've told Al a million times to keep this thing locked," she said. Then she wagged her finger at Penny. "Guns are very dangerous. Now promise me you'll stay away from this cabinet."

"I promise," Penny replied, appropriately penitent.

"Good." Mrs. Schuyler smiled warmly. "Now let's go finish that gingerbread."

CHAPTER 16

The next morning, when Penny went down to the Albrights' house, the front door was open, and so she walked right in.

Cardboard boxes were stacked all along the entryway. They had been neatly labeled with thick black Magic Marker: "Baby Clothes." "Wedding Box." "Winter Sweaters."

"I'm not letting that criminal drive us out of this house!" Mr. Albright roared, his voice carrying to where Penny was standing. "We are not the Wine-gartens! We are not running away from a kid!"

"Well, I've had it! Do you hear me?" Mrs. Albright shouted back, her voice breaking.

Penny was astonished. She had never heard Mrs. Albright yell at Mr. Albright.

There was a long moment of silence, and then the

sound of china shattering rang through the house.

"Now look what you did!" Mrs. Albright cried, sounding close to tears. "That was Becky's baby cup! It's ruined."

"Mom, it's okay," Benji's voice said beseechingly. "Look, I'll bet I can fix it."

Penny stepped into the doorway of the kitchen. "Uh, hi."

Mrs. Albright stood on a high stool before the open cabinet. The top shelf was empty, and the table was stacked with plates wrapped in newspaper. Mr. Albright was glaring at his wife, and Benji was frozen, crouching next to the shattered cup on the floor.

"What's going on?" Penny asked.

Mr. Albright looked hard at his wife. She put her face in her hands and started sobbing softly.

"We're moving," Benji said in a dull voice.

"Moving?" Penny asked in a hollow voice. *Moving?*

"We are not moving! Why should we run and hide when that monster's the one who did this!" Mr. Albright shouted, his face reddening, pointing furiously in the direction of the Devlins' house. Penny could smell the beer on his breath from where she stood.

"Because I can't take it anymore!" Mrs. Albright wailed, and threw down the mug she was holding, smashing it on the floor. Penny knew that mug. She remembered drinking hot chocolate with marshmallows from it.

Mr. Albright turned and stalked out of the kitchen, slamming the front door so hard it shook the house.

Mrs. Albright visibly tried to get herself under control. "Don't mind him, Penny." A shuttered look came over Mrs. Albright's face, and she said, in a deliberately bright voice, "I think we need a change of scenery. I'd like to be closer to my parents. They live in New Jersey. We'll only be a few hours away. And you can visit us anytime you want."

Penny looked at Benji, met his stricken eyes, and said, "Great."

Penny wandered home and went up to her bedroom.

She felt sick to her stomach. Things were never going to be the same. Not now. Not with Benji leaving. She kept playing the words over and over in her mind. Benji was moving.

She lay on the bed, staring up at the canopy, and felt

a wave of exhaustion swamp her. She hadn't been sleeping much lately. Her eyes fluttered shut, and she felt herself drift off. And then someone was shaking her shoulder softly. She rolled away from the hand, but it kept shaking her insistently. She peeped out through narrowed lids. And then her eyes widened in horror.

Becky stood by the side of the bed, wearing the white cotton eyelet dress, her face a waxy mask, blood dripping down her neck and pooling on the pink carpet.

"Penny, why are you being so mean to me?" Becky whispered, reaching out a hand to her.

Penny flinched, screaming, and then someone was shaking her hard and she blinked to see her mom standing over her.

"Penny! It's just me. Mom!"

Penny stared wordlessly at her mother.

"Are you okay, sweetie? Were you having a nightmare?"

Penny nodded mutely, and her mother smoothed back her sweat-matted hair.

"Why don't you go splash some water on your face and then come downstairs. I have to go to the grocery store, and I need someone to help me with all the bags and the baby."

"Sure," Penny said shakily.

Penny shepherded Baby Sam around the store while her mother took the cart and shopped. The baby was being good, just looking around at all the shapes and bright colors and listening to the sounds. He reached for a can of tomato paste, and Penny gave it to him. He clutched it in his grubby, fat hands, gurgled happily, and immediately started to gnaw on it. Penny pushed his stroller along, pausing in front of the comic-book rack. She was flipping through a comic book when she saw them.

Mr. and Mrs. Devlin.

The Devlins were older parents, in their late fifties. Mrs. Devlin sat slumped in a wheelchair, wearing a faded housedress. She had lost so much weight, it looked like she could blow away. Her skin was paper-thin, stretched taut over her bones. Mr. Devlin was tall and heavyset, with a resigned sadness etched around his eyes, as if all the blows life had dealt him had finally taken their toll.

Penny craned her head to look at their purchases.

They were buying bananas, crackers, and ginger ale. Sick food.

They didn't even know that their son was lying dead in the creek.

Bile rose in the back of Penny's throat, and the image of Caleb's dead body flashed before her eyes.

Mr. Devlin saw Penny staring at him, pale and wide-eyed, and gave her a tired smile.

"Honey, will you go out to the shed and see if there is any charcoal?" Penny's mother asked when they had returned home. "I forgot to buy some, and I don't want to have to go out again. It's almost six thirty and I haven't even started dinner."

The shed was in the back corner of the yard, bordering the woods, and it was where her father kept the lawnmower, sleds, and other junk. Sure enough, Penny found half a bag of briquettes at the back, near a pile of mouse droppings. She was closing the door to the shed when she heard the yipping.

Standing at the edge of the dark woods was Buster, caked from head to toe in mud.

"Hey there, Buster," Penny said. He jumped up, his feet scrambling at her legs. She bent down and he licked her face, as if grateful to finally be back in civilization after what had clearly been an adventure. He yipped at her and wiggled his tail.

"Boy, are you in big trouble," Penny said, shaking her head. She grabbed the dog and carried him around the side of the house and across the street to the Bukvics'. She hesitated a moment before knocking, just listening.

"Amy!" Mrs. Bukvic's voice demanded furiously. "Where do you think you're going, young lady? You know you're grounded."

"You can't ground me for the rest of my life—it's not fair!"

"Well, that's too bad. You don't have the sense that God gave you. How could you even think of dating Caleb when you know what he did to that little girl? And what about Buster?"

"What do you know? Leave me alone!"

"What were you thinking, running around with someone as dangerous as Caleb Devlin in the first place?"

"You don't know anything!"

Penny knew that the police had been by to question Amy.

"Don't you talk to me like that!" Mrs. Bukvic shouted.

"You're ruining my life!" Amy screamed.

"Amy!" Mrs. Bukvic called.

Suddenly the door flew open and Amy stood there, her eyes red-rimmed. Mrs. Bukvic appeared behind her, framed in the doorway.

"Um, hi," Penny said awkwardly, looking down at the muddy dog cradled in her arms. "I found Buster."

Buster yipped happily.

There was a moment of shocked silence, and then Amy turned and shot her mother a triumphant look.

She pushed past Penny and ran out the door and up the block.

Later that night, Penny sat at the desk in her bedroom, reviewing a list she had drawn up of possible suspects, scribbling down notes. The police still believed Caleb was the killer, and continued to search for him. They'd even looked in the woods, checking out his old haunts. She'd watched from a distance as they'd walked methodically through the trees. If they'd only looked down into the creek, they would have seen his rotting body lying there and known the truth.

But they hadn't.

"What are you doing?" Teddy asked, opening the door and limping in like he owned the room. He was wearing his pajamas.

"Teddy! Get out. Don't you ever knock?"

"No," Teddy said, confused, steadying himself on his crutches. "Why are you acting so weird?"

She flipped her pad over.

"What are you doing?"

"Nothing," she said, walking casually over to the bed and flopping down on her belly. He immediately hobbled over to her desk and picked up the pad.

"Put that down!" she ordered him, leaping up and rushing over.

"What's this?"

"I told you. Nothing," she hissed, tugging on the pad.

But Teddy was already reading the list. "Why do you have all these names here?"

"Nothing," she said in a terse voice.

"You really don't think Caleb killed Becky?" Teddy said, a look of shock dawning on his face.

She said nothing.

"But Caleb killed Becky!" he insisted in a shaken voice.

"How do we know for sure?"

Teddy gestured emphatically. "Because everybody says so!" He looked at her closely. "Aren't you scared of him?"

"I was. I mean, I am," she amended herself. "But how do we know he killed Becky? How do we know for sure?"

"What about me?" he said, holding up his cast.

"Teddy," she said gently. "Maybe he just found you."

"He did it! He was laughing at me! I remember!"

"You don't know that for sure—"

Teddy stood up, clearly distraught. "You're wrong."

"Teddy—"

"You're wrong!" he shouted defiantly, and limped quickly out of the room.

The next afternoon, Penny's mother cornered her just as she was leaving the house.

"Have you seen Mr. Cat lately?" her mother asked.

Penny paled, thinking fast. "Yeah, he was chasing this squirrel in Mac's backyard but wouldn't come when I called him."

"That cat." And then her mother narrowed her

eyes. "Where are you going?"

"To play with the guys. Why?"

"I just want to know where you're going to be, that's all. That's part of the deal with me being a mom. Things are very tense right now, Penny."

Her mother took her hand, rubbing it in a soothing gesture. "Believe me, I never thought something like this would happen, either. That's the whole reason we moved here in the first place. But I guess bad people don't just live in cities. Caleb's a scary boy. It's okay to be worried."

"Uh, I'm not worried," Penny stammered. Not much to worry about from a dead boy. She had more to fear from the living.

"But you seem to be having a lot of nightmares. And what about these panic attacks? Your dad and I thought you'd grown out of them, but Mrs. Albright told me you had one the night of the haunted trail. That's not good. And Nana said that you were pretty upset when you called her."

Penny went still. What else had Nana told her mother? How much had Penny said to Nana? She couldn't remember.

Finally Penny said, "I guess you're sort of right. I

guess I am worried about Caleb. You know, Becky."

"Well, that's perfectly natural," her mother said, pleased with the answer. "You know you can tell me anything."

Penny looked at her mother and thought: *Really, Mom, anything? Can I tell you that there's a dead boy rotting in the creek and that I killed him? Can I tell you how I need to find the real killer so that the boy rotting in the creek will get out of my head?*

"I know," Penny said.

Her mother smiled in relief. "I'm so glad we had this little talk."

"Me too," Penny said, then turned and went out to the garage to get her bicycle.

She biked up the block and waited at the top of Lark Hill Road for the guys, wondering if she was any closer at all to catching the real killer.

Zachary came huffing slowly up the slope of the hill.

"Hey, Penny!" he shouted, his eyes brightening when he saw her.

"How's it going?" she asked with a smile.

"Pretty good," he said, pausing to wipe a trickle of sweat off his forehead.

Oren wheeled up a moment later.

"Where's Mac?" Penny asked.

Oren squinted into the sun. "The dentist, I think."

"The dentist? Didn't he just go a few weeks ago?" Penny asked.

"Yeah, he's been going to the dentist a lot," Oren said with a shrug.

"That's weird." Penny flipped her bike around. "Look, I'll go check his house and meet you at the store."

Mrs. McHale's station wagon was sitting in the driveway. Penny had raised a hand to knock on the front door when she heard Mac shouting.

"I'm not going!"

"Angus, stop screaming," Mrs. McHale said soothingly.

"I don't want to go! All that guy does is ask me how I feel, and I don't feel like going!"

"Well, I don't care. Either you go or it's Catholic school for you. It's not up to me! I'm missing work for this, you know!"

"But I already told Amy I was sorry!"

"Well, it's not up to her, either. You're going to have to be a grown-up about this."

"I don't care!" Mac roared, and then a door slammed. Penny ducked down and watched as Mac tore out of the garage on his bike, pedaling away hard.

Penny stood there and thought, *What was that about?* It seemed that even Mac had a deep, dark secret. Fear pooled uneasily in her stomach. She instinctively knew that asking Mac about this would be hazardous to her health. If he was the murderer, he'd kill her for asking too many questions. And if he wasn't, he'd probably just beat her up.

There was only one person she could ask.

Amy.

Penny found her sitting on the Lark Hill bridge, legs dangling over the dry creek, smoking a cigarette.

"Hey," Penny said.

Amy nodded curtly and held out her cigarette, an unspoken challenge.

Penny surprised herself by taking it and drawing deeply. The smoke tickled her lungs, and she started coughing violently. Amy slapped her hard on the back.

"Relax," Amy said, laughing, not unkindly.

Penny's eyes were wet with tears. And then she

started laughing, too.

Amy grinned at her, taking the cigarette back and puffing out smoke rings. "Remember that time we were spying on Mrs. McHale and that mechanic she was dating and you started wheezing and she threatened to call the cops? Man, she is something else. No wonder Mac's screwed up, the way she's always bringing all those guys home."

Penny nodded.

They sat there for a moment in companionable silence. It was so weird, Penny thought. It was almost as if Caleb's death had brought them closer together. Except, of course, for the little fact that Amy had no idea that Caleb was dead.

"You okay?" Penny asked tentatively.

For a split second Amy's face looked vulnerable, and then she glanced away. "I guess. Hasn't been the greatest to find out my boyfriend's wanted by the cops for murder." She said this as if it was an annoyance, like not getting her driver's license on the first try.

Penny prodded her. "Do you think Caleb really killed Becky? I mean, you knew him, *really* knew him."

Amy met Penny's steady gaze. "No. He would never. He . . ." Here her voice trailed off as she stared into the distance for a minute. "He was really messed up when he was a kid, you know, back when he was sent away." She shook her head vehemently. "But not now. He told me that place was a living nightmare, that he'd never do anything ever again that would get him sent back there. There's just no way."

"I don't think so, either," Penny said simply.

"You don't?" Amy asked in an astonished voice.

"Who do you think did it?"

Amy worried her lip. "I don't know."

"What about Mac? What happened between you two?"

Amy scrunched up her eyes. "That kid is a total freak."

"What do you mean?"

She inhaled deeply and then raised her pinky to smooth her lipstick. "He was spying in my bedroom window, watching me get dressed. What a disgusting creep."

"Is that why he's seeing a doctor?"

Amy shrugged.

A red Trans Am roared down Lark Hill Road, screeching to a stop next to them. Penny was so startled, she almost fell off the bridge.

The car idled there for a moment, and then

the window rolled down.

Penny flinched, half expecting Caleb's pale eyes to appear.

"Come on," Doug Coles said impatiently, his greasy hair tied back in a ponytail.

Amy took her time, elaborately grinding out her cigarette with the heel of her shoe.

"Where are you going?" Penny whispered.

Amy's face hardened. "None of your business," she said, her eyes flinty now.

She walked over to the car and got in without a backward glance.

The boys were sitting on the curb in the cul-de-sac, comparing baseball trading cards. Swapping and flipping them around.

"Man, the Phillies blow," Mac said in a disgusted voice, throwing down a pile of cards.

"I like the Phillies," Teddy said loyally.

"You can have all of mine if you give me your Yankees cards," Mac said, with a sly look.

Teddy hesitated. "I don't know."

Penny sat down next to Zachary. "Hey," she said.

He grinned at her.

"Did you guys know that Amy Bukvic gets undressed in front of her bedroom window?" Penny announced.

Mac's eyes narrowed.

Oren hooted. "No way. You mean I can see those melons of hers anytime?"

"What melons?" Teddy asked, confused.

Benji poked him in the ribs. "Her boobs, man."

"Her boobs?" Teddy echoed, a look of shock on his face.

Oren grinned. "They're as big as real watermelons."

"More like cantaloupes," Zachary said, squeezing the air.

"Or grapefruit," Teddy offered, eager to be part of this grown-up boys' game.

Benji looked at Penny and shook his head, smiling.

"What do you think, Mac?" Penny asked pointedly. "Watermelons or cantaloupes or grapefruit?"

"What are you trying to say, huh, Penny?" Mac asked, his voice low and threatening.

The boys stared at Mac.

"What's going on?" Benji asked.

"Ask Mac," Penny challenged, looking directly at Mac.

Mac stood up and walked over to her, his skin glistening with sweat. She suddenly realized how much bigger he was than her.

"Whoa, whoa," Oren said, stepping between Mac and Penny.

Mac stared at Penny for one long minute and then stalked off, up the block.

"What was that about?" Benji asked.

Penny released a held-in breath. "Nothing."

"Anybody want some gum?" Zachary offered, eager to restore normalcy to the little group.

"I'll take some," Penny said.

"You got it," he said cheerfully. He dug around in his pants and pulled out a stick. It was warm from being in his pocket, and already soft. Penny put it in her mouth anyway.

"Thanks," she said, chewing.

Something fell out of Zachary's pocket and bounced onto the street. Penny and Zachary reached for it at the same time, but Penny got it. She looked at it for a minute. A marble.

"It's pretty," she said.

Penny stared at the marble resting in her palm. It was bright solid red, an unusual color. She was used to seeing blues and greens. The glass marble glinted in the late-afternoon sun. Now where had she seen that before? It looked so familiar to her. That strange glowing red.

Zachary eyed her warily.

The image of a scorpion popped unsummoned into her mind, and Nana's words came rushing back to her.

Scorpions like to live near you, where they can do you the most harm.

The creek. Red eyes.

Mr. Cat.

She met Zachary's still eyes and knew.

CHAPTER 17

Penny stood up abruptly, hovering over her little brother protectively.

"Teddy," Penny said in a deceptively calm voice. "It's time to go home for dinner."

"Now? But Mom didn't call us yet," he said, squinting at her through his glasses.

"Well, it's dinnertime, so let's go," Penny said stiffly, grabbing his hand almost roughly.

Penny jerked Teddy up, sending his baseball cards flying.

"Hey! Now look what you did!" Teddy said, scrambling down awkwardly to pick up the cards.

Benji raised an eyebrow at Penny.

"Here," Zachary said, getting down on the ground to help Teddy pick up the cards.

"Thanks," Teddy said in a grateful voice, a voice that

said he didn't know why his sister was acting so weird.

"Come on," she urged, shoving his crutches into his hands.

"Man," Teddy groused, following her reluctantly.

"We'll see you after dinner," Oren said.

"Yeah," Benji said. "Meet us back here and then we'll head down to the fort."

"Okay," Teddy called.

Penny walked purposefully up the block, half pushing her little brother.

"Quit it!" he said, wrenching himself away. "What's your problem?"

"Nothing," she said, and looked back.

Zachary was staring at them, an odd expression on his face.

"But he killed Becky!"

Penny paced back and forth on the kitchen floor, her dinner untouched. Her parents kept telling her to slow down, but she couldn't—every minute was another minute that Zachary was out there. She had to make them understand.

"Penny," her mother said. "You can't go around saying these things. It's inflammatory."

"But you gotta believe me! It really is Zachary! I

found the marble!" Penny said.

"The marble?" her father asked, confused.

"Zachary killed Mr. Cat and stuffed him and put marbles in his eyes!"

"Mr. Cat's dead?" her mother asked in a bewildered voice. "I thought you said you just saw him chasing squirrels in Mac's backyard?"

"I didn't! I made that up! He's dead!"

"But why do you think Mr. Cat's dead, honey? He probably just wandered off, the way he always does. He'll turn up eventually," Mrs. Carson soothed.

"He won't turn up! He's dead! I saw his body!"

"His body?"

Penny didn't care; she knew it was going to sound stupid. "I saw his body at the creek, and when I went to show the boys, it was gone!"

Teddy looked up from his plate and rolled his eyes.

"Mr. Cat might have been sleeping," her father said reasonably. "And then he ran off."

"He was *dead*, Dad."

"You were at the creek?" her mother asked in a horrified voice. "What were you doing at the creek? I thought I told you—"

"Zachary's the one, Mom!" Penny wailed in frustration.

"Phil," her mother murmured.

"Now Penny," her father said gently.

"Can I be excused please?" Teddy asked, already pushing away from the table.

"Yes," Mrs. Carson said, pushing her own chair back. "I better go pick up Sam from Mrs. Schuyler."

"No, Dad!" Penny shouted, knowing what was at stake here. "We have to call the police. He's gonna hurt somebody else! I know it! He already killed Becky! See, I talked to Amy about Caleb and——"

Her mother interrupted her. "Wait a minute. You talked to Amy and she told you that Zachary was the killer?"

"You don't understand!"

Her mother gave her a level look. "Penny, you know how mean Amy is to you. It's not beneath her to tell you a lie. She's probably doing this to upset you."

"I *am* upset! Zachary's going to kill someone else, I just know it!" she said, her voice rising.

"But how do you know?" her father asked.

"Because of the marble! Don't you see? It's been him all along! He's been leaving clues. He knew everyone would think it was Caleb. And he was right!"

Out of the corner of her eye, she saw a small figure, a blur. Teddy. He was hobbling out through the laundry room door to the garage. He was going to meet the boys in the cul-de-sac.

"Teddy!" Penny called. "Wait!"

But it was too late—he was gone, and her father was talking to her.

"Penny," her father said almost sternly. "Even the police think it's Caleb. That's why they're looking so hard for him."

There was a loud banging on the front door.

Mr. Schuyler stood on their porch, holding a rifle and looking shaken. "Doc, you gotta come quick. Bud Albright's going nuts. Got himself drunk and got some crazy ideas in his head. He's over at the Devlins' with his twelve-gauge, threatening to shoot up the house. One way or another we're gonna need a doctor over there."

Her father paled. "Someone called the cops?"

"What good are they?" Mr. Schuyler asked.

Mrs. Carson gave an exasperated sigh. "I better call them now."

"But Caleb didn't kill Becky!" Penny insisted. She almost shouted: *It's not him because he's rotting in the creek!*

Mr. Schuyler stared at her in confusion. "What?"

"Penny, not now," her father said distractedly.

She grabbed her father's arm, tugging him. "Please,"

...eaded. "You've got to believe me. We have to ... him."

Her parents exchanged a worried look.

"Penny," her mother said sharply. "Calm down."

"It's Zachary!" Penny shrieked, having worked herself into a frenzy in the face of their total disbelief. "It's—"

Mr. Schuyler looked startled. "Zachary? That chubby boy?"

"Penny—" her mother said, her face stricken.

"—Zachary!" And suddenly it was too much, she couldn't take it anymore. All the fear and stress of the past few weeks came barreling down, and Penny felt her chest go tight, and a light-headed feeling washed over her, and then her fingers were tingling, her lips going numb, and she couldn't catch her breath.

For a moment both of her parents just looked at her, and she saw it on their faces: fear for the hysterical daughter who couldn't breathe, who was losing her mind.

"Sweetie, slow down. Take nice even breaths. You're having a panic attack," her dad said in his doctor's voice.

"Penny, slow down, here's a bag," her mother said, putting a brown paper bag into her hands. Penny put it over her mouth.

CHAPTER 18

Penny struggled up from the hazy depths of black-
ness, the world a swirl around her.

She sat up quickly, but the motion jolted her stomach and she almost threw up. She collapsed back on
the bed, looking up at the canopy spinning fuzzily
above her, like some magnificent amusement park
ride. With an effort, Penny turned her head to look
out the window. The sky looked darker. The clock on
the bedside table swam in her vision, unreadable. No,
there it was, she hadn't been out for long. What had
her father given her?

She counted to ten and then tried again, manag-
ing to sit up on the edge of the bed. *Get up,* she told
herself, one foot on the rug and then the other. The
pink rug seemed to swirl around like a whirlpool,
its tendrils reaching for her like the tentacles on a

sea anemone. She shook herself. *Get up and call the police before Zachary kills Teddy!*

Tentatively, one step at a time, she maneuvered her way down the hall, weaving back and forth, using the wall to guide her. She had no sense of distance or depth, and the hall seemed to go on forever, like that ride in the fun house, the one where the tunnel keeps getting longer, the door at the other end farther and farther away.

When she reached the stairs and looked down, she started to shake. They seemed utterly terrifying, impossibly steep. There was no way she could walk down them. She got on her rear end and slid down the carpeted steps, one at a time, as she used to do when she was a small child.

Finally she was at the bottom. She sat still for a moment, listening for the voices of her parents, but the house was quiet, with only the cranky sound of the air conditioner laboring in the background. She stood up shakily, her vision fuzzy, and navigated the dark, windowless hall to the kitchen more by memory than by sight. She pulled open the French doors that led to the kitchen and closed her eyes instinctively against the bright hanging light; it hurt her eyes. She raised a hand to shield them, and when she lowered it, she peered through slit eyes and saw the vague outline of a person.

"Dad?"

And then her vision cleared, and she saw that it wasn't her dad at all.

It was Zachary.

He was holding a plastic bag, and something red was dripping from it onto the floor. Blood?

She drew in her breath. "How did you get in here?"

"The spare key. You know, the one under the rock." Zachary smiled and then, seeing her shocked expression, let his smile slip. "I biked and got Popsicles for the guys, and I got you one, too," he explained in a rush. He held out the bag. "Strawberry's your favorite, right?"

She scrambled backward, feeling sick, the kitchen wavering. "You killed Becky!" she blurted out through cottony lips.

His eyes widened in shock. "Me?"

"The marble! You have a red marble just like . . . like the one in Mr. Cat's eyes!"

He shifted from foot to foot, awkwardly. "The red marbles? Oren gave them to me."

"Oren?"

"We traded." He shrugged. "I gave him a few baseball cards."

"Oren?" Penny whispered, not wanting to believe.

"Yeah," Zachary said, setting the bag of melted Popsicles on the floor. He dug around in his pockets and pulled out a pile of stuff. "And he gave me these cool silver ones, too. He said they're from Mexico. Pretty cool, huh?" There was a tinge of excitement in his voice.

Penny walked over to the counter and slumped onto a rattan stool, her head in her hands, suddenly remembering the way Oren's eyes had narrowed when she'd told him about finding marbles in Mr. Cat's eyes. It was all falling together now. It could have been Oren chasing her in the woods that first night, and then, of course, he could have staged the guts—he was right next to her—not to mention the rat and the trap in the woods. He could even have somehow rigged the fire at the fort. What had he said?

"I can't believe he won't come home with all the stuff that's going on with Caleb! I thought he'd come home!"

He'd been doing it to get his father to come home. Only it hadn't worked. Not yet, at least.

"The guys, they're down in the woods with Oren! We gotta go!" she said urgently, standing abruptly. The kitchen seemed to close in on her, a rush of nausea slapping her so hard that she almost threw up right there.

"Whoa. You okay?" Zachary said, concern in his voice.

"I feel sick," she whispered.

"Man, you're not gonna barf, are you?" he asked worriedly.

Penny shook her head, even though she wanted to. She looked up at him and said, in an anguished voice, "Oren's the killer."

"What do you mean?" Zachary asked, wrinkling his nose.

"It's not Caleb doing all this stuff. It's Oren."

"I don't understand why you're saying all these crazy things. The guys have been talking, you know." He paused. "That policeman asked all of us who had been the last one to see Becky alive."

"What?"

"Penny," he said simply. "You were the last one to see Becky alive. You walked her out of the woods, remember?"

"But, but—" *But the policeman didn't ask me that question!* she wanted to shout. Pain sliced through her head. Did everyone think she had killed Becky? Was someone trying to frame her? Make it look like she was the kind of person who could kill—

An image of Caleb's bloated, rotting body appeared before her eyes, and she stumbled back, grabbing the stool.

Zachary held out his hands in a calming way. "Don't worry, it's cool. We didn't tell him, Penny. Everyone knows it's Caleb."

"But it's not!"

He stared at her, disbelief plain on his face.

"You don't understand," she said, slurring her words. *You don't unnderthand*. She sounded like Elmer Fudd.

"Penny," he said, shaking his head.

She stared defiantly at him. He was just like her parents. "Nobody listens!"

His round face grew gentle, his cheeks softening. "I'm listening."

"Can't tell," she whispered brokenly, the weight of Caleb's cigarette case heavy in her pocket.

Zachary's voice thrummed in her head. "Sure you can," he said encouragingly.

Sure you can.

"Caleb's dead!"

The kitchen was silent for a long moment.

"Caleb's dead?" he asked, taking a wary step back.

"I saw his body," she whispered. It felt so good to finally tell someone, to get this weight off her chest, this horrible weight that had been pushing down on her soul, dragging it to some dark place. The words spilled from her mouth. "His body, it's in the creek."

"But how? I mean, who killed him?"

Penny shrugged helplessly.

"Are you sure he's dead?"

"He's dead. His body——" Then she gulped hard and sat back down on the rattan stool, knowing her legs wouldn't support her a minute longer. "Look," she said miserably, holding out the silver cigarette case. It gleamed dully in the kitchen light.

Zachary stared at the case, transfixed.

"Why didn't you tell anyone?" he whispered.

"Because," she said, her voice catching. "Because of Becky. I knew he didn't kill Becky, and I was trying to figure out who did. And now I have. It's Oren."

Zachary looked at her and then at the bag of melting Popsicles on the floor.

"Whoa," he said, almost to himself. He picked up the bag and went over to the kitchen counter, with its sink full of dirty dinner dishes. He flipped on the faucet and looked out the window, into the backyard.

"We have to tell the police," he said. "We're just kids."

Penny sniffed miserably. "I know."

"It's gonna be okay," she heard Zachary say in a soothing voice. He was standing right in front of her with a glass of water in one hand.

And then there was a flash of silver, a glinting arc, and Penny moved instinctively, tumbling back off the stool and slamming hard onto the floor. She scrambled up, the world spinning, and pumped her feet fast, toward the French doors and the hall leading upstairs. Zachary followed her slowly, the long, pointy kitchen knife in one hand.

Zachary was shaking his head in disappointment. "Penny," he said. "Why did you have to go and do this? Everything was going so great."

"It was you all along?" she gasped.

He lunged at her with the knife. He moved pretty fast, faster than she'd ever seen him move on the softball field. She stumbled down the hall toward the stairs and scrambled up quick as she could, slipping, her balance off.

Zachary paused at the bottom of the stairs. "I was

just doing what I had to do. And it worked. Everyone thought it was Caleb, and you liked me!"

"We *do* like you," she said uncertainly.

"I just wanted to be friends with you guys!" He looked up at her, an anguished expression on his face. "You never let me get ice cream with you before all this happened!" he said, wailing.

Penny looked at him in horror.

"Why Becky?" she whispered shakily.

"It wasn't my fault. She was just so nosy, always following me. And you! You were my favorite!" he said, his face twisting. "Why'd you have to ruin everything!"

Penny felt a rush of adrenaline at these words and moved faster now, crablike up the stairs, two steps at a time, until she was nearly at the top.

"No," Penny said quickly. "I do like you, I—"

"Liar!" he roared. "You're gonna tell everybody, and then I'll never be friends with the guys! After all my hard work!"

"I won't! I promise!" Penny begged, desperately.

"No, it's too late," Zachary said sadly, pointing the shiny knife at her, the same knife her mother used to chop onions.

"Please," she started to say, and then all at once she knew there was no use talking because he was nuts, absolutely bananas, and with that thought she started down the upstairs hall, hearing him barreling up the stairs behind her. She flung the door to her bedroom open and staggered in, falling to her knees and rolling under her bed.

A moment later, she saw Zachary's feet enter the room, watched them circle the bed. There was a vicious tearing noise and clumps of stuffing rained down to the floor, along with a lone plush bear arm. Georgie.

Penny rolled out from the other side of the bed, and Zachary caught sight of her. He flung himself at her, knife raised, her worst nightmare come true. Penny grabbed her pillow and held it out to shield herself. The knife ripped through the fabric, and feathers went flying. Penny shoved the pillow at Zachary and pushed with all her might. He tumbled onto the bed and she rushed back into the hall.

The door to her parents' bedroom was open, and she slipped in. She heard loud voices and wild shouting outside, and crossed the room to the open window to look out. A crowd of parents had gathered in front of the Devlins' house—her mother and father were right there, too—and she couldn't quite see, but there seemed to be some sort of commotion. The shouting was getting louder.

"Mom! Dad!" she screamed hysterically out the window, her voice shaking with the effort. "Help!"

But at that exact moment a loud shot rang out. And the shouting grew to a steady roar, punctuated by someone's high-pitched screams.

Nobody could hear her.

"Penny?" Zachary called in a frustrated voice.

Penny shook her head. A wave of nausea washed over her, and she fell to her knees on the other side of her parents' bed.

There was a soft noise at the door, and Penny flattened herself against the floor, hoping her body was obscured by the bed. She closed her eyes tight, her slender body wracked by shivers. Zachary seemed to hesitate a moment and then moved off down the hall, calling her name.

"Penny?"

Penny drew herself together, her heart pounding. She just wanted to curl up in a ball and hide under her parents' bed as she used to do when she was a small child and played with Teddy, their favorite game, hide-and-seek. *Hide-and-seek, that was it. Just pretend it's a game*, she thought. He was on *her* territory. Even half blind, she knew it better than he did. But where to go? Her parents' bedroom looked soft, all the edges blurred. And then there, in the corner, she saw the door.

The attic.

She crawled quietly across the floor and tried to open the door with a tug, but it was sticky; it wouldn't budge.

"Come on," she hissed urgently, pulling hard, frantically. The door finally gave way with a small creak. She rushed in, flicked on the light, and closed the door, looking for a way to lock it, but of course there was nothing, because why would someone lock an attic from the inside? She heard Zachary calling her name and climbed up the stairs.

"Penny."

The attic was stuffy and smelled like hot, stale wood. Penny took stock of her surroundings: the cotton-candy insulation, the boxes of baby clothes, the old wicker stroller with the sheet draped over it. Hanging from rods attached to wooden beams were the garment bags, big ones, the old-fashioned kind made of thick, sturdy reinforced plastic and containing years' worth of old clothes and Halloween costumes. The bags were big—big enough to hold an entire wardrobe.

Or a slender girl.

She heard the footsteps enter the bedroom below and gently tugged the pull chain hanging from the bare bulb at the peak of the roof, plunging the attic into darkness.

CHAPTER 19

She felt a tickle in her nose. *Please,* she prayed silently, *please don't let me start sneezing.*

"I know you're in here somewhere," Zachary called from the bottom of the stairs. She heard him click the light switch on and off a few times, but the light did not go on.

"That's not going to help you," he said, starting up the stairs.

He moved toward a stack of boxes and lifted up a sheet, peering closely in the dim light spilling through the attic vents.

She couldn't help it. She sneezed, a soft, muffled sound.

Zachary straightened up like a cat and whipped his head around, zoning in on one of the garment bags hanging from the rafters. "There you are," he said in a pleased-sounding voice.

Penny held her breath.

Zachary stepped back, raised the kitchen knife, and plunged it furiously into the garment bag again and again, the force of his fury concentrated in short, angry, stabbing strokes, a frenzy now. The sound of tearing fabric filled the attic. And then abruptly he stopped, as if all the anger had gone out of him.

He took a deep breath, as if to say he was glad *that* was over, and unzipped the bag, pushing back a thick bundle of old Halloween costumes.

There was no one inside.

Penny rushed at him from around the other side of the bag, where she had been hiding all along, and pushed him as hard as she could toward the exposed insulation. He flailed and tumbled face-first into the pink fluff, roaring like a bear stung by nettles.

But Penny wasn't about to wait for him to get up. She moved on rubbery legs to the attic stairs, but she misjudged the steepness of the first step, and the next thing she knew she was flying down the stairs, tumbling, hitting every hard, uncarpeted edge. She banged right into the door leading to the bedroom, knocking it open and landing with a hard thump on the bedroom floor, blood streaming from her nose, a huge bloody gash on her forehead, her ankle twisted, her whole body throbbing in pain.

The boys were standing there, stunned expressions on their faces.

"Holy—" Benji said.

"Penny?" Teddy asked with a horrified look on his face.

Penny started sobbing. Benji rushed to help her up, and she winced in pain.

"What happened?" he asked, alarmed.

Penny clutched Benji with all her strength, gripping him with both hands. "Zachary's up there! He killed Becky!"

Teddy looked around at the other boys. "See? That's what she was saying before!"

Benji held her away from him, looking her in the eye. She swayed in his grip, her face all splotchy, her pupils dilated, her words slurring together.

"You've completely lost your marbles," Mac said in a disparaging voice.

"I'm not lying!" she cried. "He's up there, and he's going to kill us. He told me he killed Becky," she said, looking at Benji, willing him to believe her. Benji *had* to believe her.

"Caleb killed Becky!" Mac said harshly.

"It was Zachary! He's been doing it all along and making it look like it's Caleb!"

"You've got to be kidding," Mac guffawed. "Zachary?"

"We don't have time to argue," she said urgently. "He's up there!"

"I'm sure," Mac said. His voice dripped sarcasm.

"Look, the only way to solve this is to go up there and check it out," Benji said.

"But what if Penny's right?" Oren asked uncertainly.

"Yeah," Teddy echoed.

The boys regarded one another warily.

Mac gave a disgusted snort and said, "What a bunch of wusses."

"No!" Penny shouted, throwing herself at him, her ankle hurting. "He'll kill you!"

Mac gave Penny a little push, and she fell back onto the quilt on her parents' bed. "Chill out." He turned to the other boys and said, in a voice that brooked no refusal, "Come on."

Penny watched as the boys started up the dark stairs.

"Woo-hoo, killer!" Mac called facetiously.

"Something's wrong with the light switch," she heard Oren say in a nervous voice.

"There's a pull chain upstairs. Try that," Teddy said, the sound of his cast bumping as he started hopping up the steps behind the other boys.

"Got it," Mac called down, and Penny saw yellow light spill down the stairwell.

"Whoa!" Teddy yelped.

Penny heard her little brother's voice and knew what she had to do. She forced herself to get up and limp to Teddy's bedroom. Lying on the floor next to his bed was his Louisville Slugger bat, the same bat she'd used countless times in softball. She grabbed up the comforting weight of it, and a moment later she was creeping up the stairs, pain lancing her ankle.

The boys were gathered around Zachary, looking at him—the skin of his face was red and irritated.

"Man, what happened to you?" Benji asked.

"Penny's crazy!" Zachary warbled. "She's gone nuts!"

"What'd you do to my sister?" Teddy demanded.

"I was just defending myself! She came after me!" Zachary insisted.

"But you're like twice her size," Oren said suspiciously.

"When I told her about the cops questioning us about who had been the last to see Becky alive, and that we knew that it was her, she flipped out. She said that she'd *had* to kill Becky, whatever that means. I know, it's nuts, but you know how weird she's been acting! You said so yourself, Teddy!"

"I don't know what you're talking about," Benji said. "Becky was home for dinner."

"Look!" Zachary yelled, pointing across the room at the garment bags. "Look at that bag. She tried to stab me to death with a knife!"

All four boys walked across the room to the ripped-up garment bag.

"Check it out," Mac said, examining the ragged tears, the boys huddled around him doing the same.

"This is just crazy," Oren said, sounding bewildered.

"But Penny hates knives," Benji said suddenly. "She has a thing about them, remember?" His eyes met Mac's for a long, quiet minute.

The boys turned slowly around.

Zachary was standing in the middle of the room, holding the kitchen knife, his back to the door.

"If you would have just let me play with you, none of this would have happened," Zachary said mournfully.

And then he leaped at the boys.

Teddy was so scared that one of the crutches went right out from under him and he tumbled to the floor, frantically scrambling to get out of Zachary's path.

Mac bleated in surprise, flailing his arms as he tried to get away. He accidentally smacked Benji across the chest and then plowed right into a wooden beam, falling to the floor with a low moan.

Benji grunted and stumbled, the wind knocked out of him. He looked up in time to see Zachary plunge the knife into his chest and then pull it out with a sick, sucking sound. Benji cried out in pain, falling to his knees.

Zachary gasped with effort and raised his hand to stab Benji again.

Teddy's Louisville Slugger bat struck Zachary hard on the back of his neck, with all of Penny's strength and fear behind it. A look of astonishment flashed across Zachary's face, and then he collapsed.

Penny stood over Zachary, shaking, with the bat dangling from her hand. Fury rushed through her veins, fury at this crazy, sick kid who had killed cats and people and terrorized an entire town. She wanted to smash him into a million pieces, pound him until there was nothing left. She raised the bat high, her muscles tense, the anger washing over her in waves.

"Penny," Oren whispered shakily.

Penny looked at Zachary, who looked strangely peaceful now, and thought of all the anger that had built up behind that innocent face, all the anger and frustration and hate that had turned him into a monster. She couldn't go there, couldn't allow this hungry fury to sweep her there, too, to that dark place. She would be just like him.

A monster.

And then she saw Benji, lying still on the floor, blood pooling on his chest, and rushed over.

"No," Penny whispered, starting to shake all over at the sight of Benji's waxy face, so still, the way Becky's had been, his chest bright as a valentine.

The adults burst in.

"What is going on?" Penny's mother demanded. "We heard screaming halfway down the block!"

"Benji!" Mrs. Albright screamed, rushing over to her son.

"He's dead," Penny whispered, a stunned expression on her face.

"Dead?" her father demanded, pushing the kids out of the way to get to the boy.

Mr. Albright, red-faced and wild-eyed, pushed through the doorway, toting a shotgun. Mr. Schuyler crowded in behind him anxiously, carrying his rifle.

"Where is he?" Mr. Albright cried. "Where's Caleb?"

Even now they were blaming Caleb, Penny thought. A dead boy riddled with maggots.

"It wasn't Caleb!" she shouted, overwhelmed by the ridiculousness of it all.

"Not Caleb?" Mr. Albright spat contemptuously.

Penny whirled on them in righteous fury, an avenging angel. "It was Zachary! It was Zachary all along!"

"Zachary?" Mr. Albright asked, startled.

"Yes!" she hissed, pointing at Zachary, who was starting to come around now and was groaning audibly.

"But Caleb—" Mrs. McHale said, her hands twisting.

"I tried to tell you!" Penny shouted.

The parents blanched.

"We're the kids! You *told* us it was Caleb!" Penny cried, anguished.

Her mother said, "Penny—"

"I listened to you!" Penny choked out, tears running down her cheeks, watching as her father worked furiously on Benji's lifeless body. "I listened! But you were all wrong, and now Benji's dead, too," she said, her voice breaking.

"No, not my boy," Mr. Albright said, stricken, dropping his shotgun to the floor.

And then Penny couldn't take it anymore. She fell to her knees, her face in her hands. She didn't even want to live, not anymore, not knowing that Benji was dead. It was too much. Her slender body shook with the force of her sobs.

"It's okay, Janine," her father said to Mrs. Albright, holding his hands, wet with blood, firmly over Benji's chest.

Penny went still. She looked up.

Her father smiled weakly. "He's got a pulse."

The sounds of approaching sirens filled the air.

CHAPTER 20

When the rain finally came, it fell hard, viciously. Buckets and buckets poured down, clogging gutters, flooding basements. The kids sat inside, playing endless games of cards, counting every inch that fell, watching the weatherman talk about how much more they could expect. It was the biggest rainfall in years; if it kept up, they were going to have to call in the National Guard, because creeks and rivers were rising. All people could talk about was the rain and, of course, Zachary Evreth, who had been packed off to a mental hospital in western Pennsylvania.

It finally stopped raining in the early hours of the morning, the sun breaking out brightly, almost guiltily, it seemed. Penny flew out of the house and down into the woods. She ran through the mud and muck, completely ruining her new white sneakers. She didn't care, she had to see. She fell three times, and when she reached the creek, she was covered in mud.

She stopped at the cliff's edge, took a deep breath, and looked down at the place where Caleb's body had been.

But all she saw was muddy rushing water, thick as chocolate.

Later that day, Penny and the boys were biking down Lark Hill Road when they saw the flashing lights of a police car, and an ambulance, too. A small crowd had gathered by the fieldstone bridge.

"What's going on?" Oren asked.

"You kids don't want to see this," Officer Cox said, trying to wave them away.

"See what?" Teddy asked automatically. His cast was off, and he wore a brace on his foot, with a long sock over it. Looking at him sitting on his bike, you'd never even know anything had ever happened. Even Benji was on the mend, and was going to be fine.

"Yeah, what?" Mac demanded, shoving forward to peer over the bridge.

They crowded the bridge, anxious to see. It was barely visible from above unless you were looking for it, wedged as it was between a rock and the bridge wall, the water rushing around it in swirls. But it was there all the same, and there was no mistaking it.

The bloated dead body of Caleb Devlin.

"Been here for a while, I think," Officer Cox murmured to the young cherub-cheeked officer, who looked like he was going to lose his lunch.

"Man," Teddy whispered under his breath.

Officer Cox shook his head sadly, looked at Penny, and said, "Must've been that Evreth boy who did this, too."

But Penny Carson just nodded.

And then she got on her bike and rode away.

Read Jennifer L. Holm's BOSTON JANE adventures!

BOSTON JANE: An Adventure
Hc 0-06-028738-1
Pb 0-06-440849-3

When she's abandoned by her fiancé in the Pacific Northwest, sixteen-year-old Jane Peck must find the strength to survive on her own.

BOSTON JANE: Wilderness Days
Hc 0-06-029043-9
Pb 0-06-440881-7

A perilous manhunt and a blossoming romance lie ahead, as Jane struggles to make a new home for herself in the rugged nineteenth-century Washington Territory.

BOSTON JANE: The Claim
Hc 0-06-029045-5

In the final episode of this critically acclaimed trilogy, Jane Peck's old Philadelphia foes make their way to the frontier, threatening her claim on land, love, and happiness.

📖 **HarperCollins***Publishers*
www.harperchildrens.com

📖 **Harper**Trophy®
An Imprint of HarperCollins*Publishers*